TWELVE - STORIES FROM AROUND THE WORLD

POORNIMA MANCO

For my flying family, my wonderful colleagues and
friends at LHRSW and the world over.

*"Once you have tasted flight, you will forever walk the earth with your eyes
turned skyward, for there you have been, and there you will always long to
return."*
— **Leonardo da Vinci**

If you'd like a FREE story, sign up at www.poornimamanco.com/free!

CONTENTS

SAKURA

Okasan was a careful gardener. She had ensured that the cherry blossom tree in our vast garden was watered, pruned and tended to well. Tall and majestic now, it had been a mere sapling as a wedding gift to her, and in its yearly blossoms, she had seen her own contentment grow. *Otosan* and she had been a happy couple. That rare couple that spoke with their eyes, finished each other's sentences and seemed to live in their own enchanted bubble that not even us three children could penetrate.

I have inherited this tree, along with everything else - the businesses, the properties, the vast and intricate network of our family fortune.

The blossoms are a delicate pink. One falls on my lap, and I look at it lying there. Midori reaches for it and brings it up to my nose. I inhale deeply. They lie when they say that the *sakura* has no fragrance. To smell the *sakura* blossom, you have to close your eyes and open your heart.

———

It was on a bed of fallen blossoms that my heart had been awakened to love and to pain.

His kiss was like a brush of a petal against my lips. My eyes had met his, in longing and in confusion. He'd brushed the hair out of my eyes and leaned in again. My lips had parted of their own volition, letting his tongue collide with mine, to explore my mouth; to probe, feel and arouse. His fingers had caressed my face, his touch setting off a thousand little explosions in my body. His arousal mirrored mine. We'd fumbled with each other's clothes, scarcely pausing to think, hoping that the dusk would conceal our lust. Hoping that no wandering feet or prying eyes would find us, limbs entwined, gorging on one another with an insatiable urgent desire.

> What a strange thing!
> to be alive
> beneath cherry blossoms

He'd quoted Kobayashi Issa when he first saw our *sakura* tree, this peculiar guest from America, this boy-man with his blue eyes and his blonde hair, and his odd way of lisping our names. *Okasan* had taken him under her wing. He was her replacement son, the boy who would substitute for Masahiko whilst he was away being Americanised. This boy who spoke Japanese with a Californian drawl that made me snigger behind his back. My sister Noriko had followed him around like a lamb, fascinated by this strange entity who had invaded our closed but happy world. I, however, had held back. Perhaps even then I had sensed how fatal he would be.

Our assignations were always set under the tree, the only place we were unobserved from the house. Just one look from him was enough to send the blood rushing to my head. His gentle exploration of my body, limb by limb. His teaching me what my own body was capable of. His watching me climax, delaying his own gratification. His amusement at my greed, at my contrastingly frantic hunger for him. His placing a *sakura* bloom behind my ear then his tongue inside, making me come unexpectedly.

Forty years of living a lie.

How can it be that memories from an age ago are as fresh as this blossom, while everything else is dried like parchment? Dried, crumpled, forgotten.

Was it in those stolen moments that I had fallen in love? In those mysterious glances that passed between us, in the beading of the sweat that lined his upper lip, in his whispered promises? We were young, it was true, but I had never felt more alive than when he held me in his arms. Alive to the possibilities of life and love.

And yet.

I had planned to follow him to America; to convince my parents to let me do what Masahiko had done before me. Such plans we had had. Such dreams. And the *kami* had laughed in their celestial abode.

Forty years of living a lie.

Why did I survive? If anyone had to perish that day, it should have been me. *Okasan*, Masahiko, Noriko - all gone in a freak boating accident. It was meant to be a fun picnic that I had instigated and then been unable to participate in. *Otosan*, who was too busy with work that day, and I, too ill to go, were the only surviving members of a once happy family. Watching *Otosan* crumpling into himself, unable to process the loss of the other half of him. And I - I, with my survivor's guilt, watching my dreamt-of future receding farther and farther away, even as the furious waves of grief and remorse knocked me down each time I tried standing up.

One never questioned duty. It was my duty to marry, to produce the heirs and to carry forward the lineage. So I did what was expected of me, breaking it off in a letter that said so little, that it said it all.

Forty years of living a lie.

————

Every Wednesday, Midori, my granddaughter visits me. She is the only one out of six grandchildren who has the time for me. We used to talk a lot when she was little: her curious little queries, her amicable silences and her silent observations reminding me of myself at her age. I would amuse her with my *origami* birds. We would lie under this tree and I would recite the *haiku* of Basho, Buson, and yes, even Issa. She still retains an affection for me, perhaps a legacy of those early days.

She humours me by bringing me to the tree every week. Even when it is not in bloom. She senses my need and indulges it with her usual grace and sensitivity which I worry might lead to great pain in her own life.

As for mine, it is nearly over. This prison of a body is letting me down gradually. I will be free of it soon, of this I am sure. Yet I will never be free of a love that I let go of voluntarily, nor the idea of the life that I might have had.

Forty years of living a lie.

Pretence and regret have been my closest companions in life. If I were to do it all over again, would I do the same? Would I submit my life to duty, denying myself the happiness of honesty and love? Maybe. Maybe not.

I let out a little grunt to tell Midori that I am ready to return to the house.

She lowers me onto the bed, shooing the *otetsudai-san* away. My eyes thank her. She leans forward and moves the hair out of them. Her touch is feather-light, reminding me momentarily of another touch from another time, long ago.

"Rest well, *Ojiisan*. I will come again next week."

She slips out of the room silently, leaving her old, paralysed grandfather to dream of blushing *sakura* and trysts with golden-haired gods.

PRECIPICE

I didn't love her then. She was just another girl, it was just another pub. Friday night, a few beers, a laugh and maybe if I got lucky, a fit bird.

She was fit all right! Her eyes, a blue that beckoned you to drown in them. Her smile, a slow sensuous curve that promised complete annihilation if you slipped. Her body ... *that* body. One night turned into two ... then a month ... and before long we were, to all intents and purposes, a couple.

I was young, ambitious and successful. I drove a Ferrari and lived in Chelsea. I had money and I was not afraid to flash it. Life had always smiled benignly on me.

She was young and ambitious too, and I was her ticket out of slavery at Gatwick Airport. Ticket Desk work, odd hours, abuse from passengers. Could one blame her?

Two months in and with our baby growing in her belly, I'd bought the biggest diamond I could afford and gotten down on one knee. Did I love her then? I cannot honestly say that I did. Yet, it seemed the right thing to do. Everyone around me was doing it. Friends and foes, coupling up, marrying their girlfriends and boyfriends, because that's what one did, right? The inevitable, expected next step that we were primed for from a young age.

The rays are filtering in through the shutters of this apartment in Marbella. They illuminate the paint peeling in the corners of the room. The colours are somewhat faded, adding to the general air of neglect and abandonment. I look at my face in the chipped mirror. The broken capillaries on my nose stand out in stark contrast to the pallor of my skin. I run my hands over my unshaven chin, wondering whether to bother with shaving or not. Then with a shrug, I walk away.

The wedding was a grand affair. The business was booming and I could afford to be lavish. Her friends oohed and aahed over the arrangements. Her mother all but swooned. My mother stood by with suppressed fury. It was all very satisfying.

She was a vision to behold as she walked down the aisle. Virginal white did become her. She looked pure and somehow ... otherworldly.

Could I have loved her just a little bit then? Possibly, very possibly.

In their room, the twins are beginning to stir. They sleep together, as closely knit at night as they are in the day. One so very blonde and sunny-natured like his mother. The other, dark and tempestuous like me. I see their little faces in repose, their cheeks still plump in toddler-hood, their eyelashes so thick and lush as they flutter with unspoken dreams. I turn away, the lump in my throat so big that it threatens to engulf me.

Coffee. I need coffee. I shuffle towards the kitchen. There is no milk. Of course! I give myself a mental head slap. I drink the coffee black. It burns a hole in my stomach.

I was there for their birth. I held her hand as she writhed and screamed. I mopped her brow as she bit down on her lip. Never was her beauty more savage than then. Never was her rage at me more potent. Yet, at the end of that long painful tunnel were these two exquisite, perfect creatures. Their tiny fingers curling around mine. Their personalities, already beginning to shine through. One bawling for her feed. The other, patiently awaiting his turn.

Mesmerised, I had held them in my arms. They were so tiny and helpless that I'd vowed to protect them with every breath in my body. I'd vowed to be the father that my old man had never been.

The birth and subsequent child-rearing had exhausted her. She was constantly tired. Tired and depressed. Her mother had stayed with us, helping with the babies and the chores. When her mother had had enough, I'd taken over, reassuring her that we'd be fine. I'd cut back on work and spent more time at home with the twins. I'd even turned away from my mother's reluctantly offered help. I wanted to be there, to be present, to do what I could. It was our little family after all. Her, me, Joe and Amy. It had a special ring to it.

Life had been good then (or was hindsight lending it a golden glow?). The business was on a roll, the recession hadn't hit yet. I was a devoted father. She was ... well, when she'd finally risen out of her apathy, an adequate mother. I had been happy. The twins had thrived. All that while she had fretted about her body, about losing her looks, and no amount of tenderness or comforting would work. Her preoccupation with something so transient, so unimportant, had confused me. Was having two healthy, beautiful babies not enough?

Not for her.

And so it had begun. Endless calorie counting. A membership at the new gym. Prohibitively expensive shoes and gear designed to make her fit in.

Little by little, she had shrunk back to her pre-pregnancy figure, diminishing, but not just in size. I tried to love her then, tried to love the mother of my children.

It's been a half-hour since she left to buy milk and other sundry groceries. I do a little mental maths, as has become a habit in the last year or so. Fifteen minutes to the store. A half-hour there. Another fifteen back. She will be back by around 10:40 a.m.

Amy stands in the doorway, sucking her thumb, staring at me. Joe stumbles in, never far behind. I scoop them up. I sing to them as I make sure they go on the potty and brush their teeth. Breakfast is a biscuit each till mum gets home. They draw silly sketches on the sheets of paper I give them. Fat crayons scribbling away furiously, their curls glinting in the sunshine, heads bowed in deep concentration.

I open the shutters and step out onto the balcony. It is a beautiful day, and the shabbiness of the apartment doesn't spoil it in the least. At the horizon, I can see the seafront, throbbing and pulsating with a life of its own. I will some of that cool breeze our way. It is warm, set to get hotter.

Can one ever pinpoint the exact moment that the rot sets in? Was it my failing business? Or my one too many beers? Was it the one and only time that I hit her? Who knows? At some point, life became a strange stage set with us cast as actors who no longer knew their lines. Indignity piled upon yet more indignity. Debt mounted, and confidence plummeted. Our rows grew louder, more strident. Friends, such as they were, melted away. Her family recoiled from the hopelessness of our situation. Mother smiled triumphantly and took a holiday abroad. I lashed out at everyone, but at her the most. At her extravagant ways, at her frivolous habits, at her preoccupation with surface gloss, her inability to be a proper wife or mother.

She was angry at first. Then she withdrew. Grew distant. The more she stepped away, the more I perversely wanted her back. I loved her now with desperate hunger. I clung to her with a juvenile delusion: my wife, for better or for worse. "It's only been worse with you," she'd sneered. And I could not dispute it. It was a demonic dance of desperation, with each of us alternately attacking or retreating. Still, we carried on pretending. Pretence, the only glue holding us together.

How soon that was to end.

The clock-watching had started accidentally, with a mate's chance remark on how long she'd been at the gym. We'd gotten through the whole pack of beer and the footie game was nearly over. I couldn't face the pity in his eyes and laughed it off. But the first stirrings of suspicion had coiled themselves around my mind.

. . .

Joe stubs his toe against a chair. His eyes, so like his mother's, fill with tears and he comes running to me. I cuddle and soothe him while Amy cries in sympathy and tries to stroke his hair.

We huddle together, like battered souls. Something inside me breaks and I start to weep as well, the helplessness of my situation hitting me afresh; the recognition that my life is just one big mess and that there is no easy way out. These great heaving sobs of their father momentarily stun the twins into silence. Then, in fright, they join in once more, our curious chorus reaching a cacophonous crescendo.

The signs were all there. The post-coital glow. The phone never out of her sight. The hastily erased texts, the long lunches, the moody silences. I just watched and hoped that she would get over this foolishness. That she would look at the innocent faces of her children and break it off. But there is none more selfish than a woman in lust.

I never confronted her. There was no need to. She grew complacent and I grew weary. Gradually, it dawned on her that I knew and her contempt for me only increased.

This was our last-ditch effort to make it work. This parody of a family vacation, this disengagement from our normal environs, this setting aside of our mutual disgust. Our willing hostages were our children: pawns in a losing game.

We had been at it for a week, trying to make this shambolic arrangement work. We'd tried to talk, sporadically emptying our thoughts but never quite baring our souls. We'd eaten meals by the seafront, to all appearances, a happy united family. We'd nursed glasses of wine by candlelight on the balcony, trying to recreate the infancy of our romance. We'd even made frantic, furious love, trying to rekindle the embers of a long-forgotten intimacy. But, each could feel the other slipping away.

Why she even tried was beyond me. Hadn't she mentioned divorce already? Divorce, with all its attendants, parading through our brief history together. Shredding all our happy memories until they were nothing but scraps in the wastelands of our minds. Ripping apart the one good thing that came out of it all - our children - ripping them from my custody and placing them with a mother who cared ... but only just, and never enough.

Why did she try? Perhaps she understood some of this. Perhaps she dreaded some of it too. Perhaps there was an iota of compassion in her. Perhaps.

Yet, last night, even that facade had come crumbling down. Her hurried whispered conversation on the balcony. Her closing with, "I love you too" had hammered in the final nail in the coffin of this union.

She'd met my eyes as she came in and I had known. Could she have sensed the desolation in me? Not so much at losing her, but losing that which was most precious to me.

My mind flitted back to that time she'd threatened me with lack of custody. Hadn't she said that she would take away my children forever because she could, because it was her word against mine and the courts would rule in her favour? Hadn't she said that she would drip so much poison into the childrens' ears that they would never want to set eyes on me again? Were these all empty threats made in the heat of the moment, or was this woman cruel enough to follow through with them?

I had heard of plenty of cases of fathers battling for visitation, fighting to regain their rightful place in their children's lives, while the mothers deliberately blocked and erased the fact of their existence. I had looked into my wife's eyes last night as she came in from the balcony, and known that none of it was beyond her.

Would I be just another statistic? Another father fighting for justice all his life?

She'd turned her back on me and retired to bed, while I'd stayed up all night pondering where my future lay.

Had there ever been love? This morning, as I viewed her through the fiery haze of my hatred, I didn't think so.

Another ten minutes or so and she'll be here. I tidy the little apartment as best as I can. Rinse my coffee cup and put it by the sink. The twins have calmed down and they sit together, playing a little game surrounded by their toys. Heads close, all hurt forgotten. Joe helps his sister dress the doll and they place her in her little carrycot, alternately cooing and giggling. The doll's vacant eyes stare at their cherubic faces, as full of life as she is bereft of it.

"Dada!" Amy commands me to my knees to help prop her other toys in a circle. In some phantasmic toy kingdom, the doll reigns with utter supremacy, mirroring Amy's growing assertiveness.

I am dry-eyed as I tear myself away from their play. The sun is rising in the sky, and the yearned-for breeze is yet to reach us. I look over the parapet of the balcony. It is a long way down. Some distance away, I see a tiny figure dressed in blue, carrying home bags loaded with groceries.

I pick up the twins. They come gladly, nestling in the familiar comfort of my arms. I climb on to the parapet, dangling my feet outwards, still holding onto them tightly. Amy squirms a bit, impatient to get back to her toys but Joe sits placidly enough, looking at me in mild curiosity, but trusting, oh so trusting!

I wait for her figure to get closer, to look up and spot us sitting on the parapet. I watch as the shopping bags fall out of her hands, as she screams and runs towards us.

I didn't love her then and I don't love her now. But I love them so much that I feel my heart will explode. I cannot let them go, I will not let them go.

It is a long way down.

CENTRAL RESERVATION

He had planned it with meticulous exactness. It was his intrinsic nature to be precise to the nth degree, to go over everything several times and then some more. The devil was in the detail after all - a long-forgotten quote from a long-forgotten time. Sometimes, if he allowed it, the other voices in his mind would try to take over. Voices that belonged to his past, voices that may have been his family, but he was never quite sure. Hurried or hushed, they would rustle like autumn leaves, colliding, colluding, questioning and discombobulating him, till he shut that trap door with a vicious thud. There was no room for doubt. The brief was clear.

He was number 398723 in the system. He couldn't recall when he had entered in his name for the draw. Perhaps he hadn't. Perhaps it had been those shadowy figures he had called Mother and Father. His recollection of the past was hazy at best. Anyway, he was in the system, and annually, he would get a reminder that his name was being entered in the draw. He would set it aside, not sure how to feel about the message. He was ninety-two already. His mind was sharp and his body not too weak. In another fifty years, that would change. At that point, he could take himself up to the Hill, and join the masses who would gas themselves into oblivion. Or, he could steal another lifetime, if his number was drawn.

He had never stolen. Or had he? He could remember being electrically shocked lightly as a child, a punishment reserved for the most minor of infractions. Was it a strawberry he had picked, unknowingly? The lesson had stayed with him. Therefore, this draw unnerved him ever so slightly. Stealing was stealing after all. And stealing someone else's life years - how was that, in any way, a good or moral thing to do?

Yet, around him were daily reminders that people did it, and lived and thrived. If you had the money and the luck of the draw, you could potentially live another fifty to a hundred and fifty odd years.

It must have cost his shadowy family a fortune to enter the draw on his behalf. Had they forfeited their own chances to allow him the possibility of a longer life? He did not know. Besides, he had absolutely no guarantee that his number would ever come up. They must have really loved him to have taken this chance, although he could remember very little of his spartan childhood. The Memory Enhancement Program he had tried a few years ago had failed. The technician kept talking of the psyche burying things too deep, and he'd lost interest after that. Yet, that trap door would, now and again, inadvertently swing open to let in a swirl of images too amorphous to latch on to, creating a deep and disturbing yearning, a sweet pain he did not know what to do with.

The message had come two months ago. He'd seen it as soon as he opened his eyes. It was etched on the ceiling.

Robert, your number has been drawn. Please contact Central Reservation at once.

With his heart thudding, he'd taken his place amongst the forty-nine other random participants in the white, sterile waiting room. He'd noticed how they all avoided each other's gaze, choosing to stare instead at the life-like characters on the 3D posters that adorned the walls - monochrome Manga art designed to distract. He'd concentrated on the girl with the large, beguiling eyes as she'd batted her lashes and flirted with him. He'd felt her giggle inside of him, and for a moment allowed himself the fantasy.

When he'd finally entered the Room, his nervousness had all but vanished, along with his qualms. The Motherboard ("call me 'Mobo'," it had said upon introduction, striving for a casual, friendly atmosphere) had done a little psychological test and then offered him the choice of three Time Zones.

"As I see it, Robert, you are not particularly ruthless by nature. Therefore you need a soft target. The downside, of course, is the fact that the number of years you steal won't be quite as many as those you get from a tougher Time Zone. Can you live with that?"

He'd ignored the irony of that question. But Mobo wouldn't recognise irony if it stood in front of her fully disrobed.

"Why have you chosen these Time Zones?"

"Well, post-2072, people started to realise what was happening. They started to build defences, to train armies and civilians for possible future attacks. Along with increased life spans and medical advances, people grew smarter and learned to anticipate how or where our attacks would come from. To steal lives from them is a task only for the very brave, the very smart, or the very foolhardy. You are none of those."

He'd agreed with that assessment, and settled randomly on 1997. He could get eighty years, give or take, if he stole from a child. A soft target. But it had to look like an accident. Or ...

The 'or' bothered him. If it all went belly-up, he would have to forfeit his remaining years to the Mobo, giving them away charitably to the Governing Body. He supposed that was how they allowed the operation to run. There was something in it for them too. How many, he wondered, had forfeited their own lives in the process of stealing another's? He didn't want to be one of those statistics.

The Mobo had presented him with a series of targets. There were infants. There were young children. There were men. There were women. But one, in particular, caught his eye and stayed with him. She was blonde and beautiful. Her shy smile captivated him, nudging open the trap door of his lost childhood, something about her reminding him of someone - was it his mother? - but his grasp on it was tenuous at best, and then it slipped away again. The Mobo stopped at her image instantly.

"You like her, Robert? She won't be an easy target, and you'll barely get fifty years out of her. Are you sure?"

"Yes," he'd muttered, his mouth dry. To steal her years would be like stealing her for himself. Stealing her unique beauty, her irrepressible charm, her shy smile, and bottling it deep inside himself. "Yes," he'd said again, "it's her."

"Then start planning, Robert. The file will be delivered to you within the hour. You have two months to prepare. And remember, it must look like an accident."

She had two sons. That should've bothered him, but strangely, it didn't. He'd immersed himself in her story, in her rise from anonymity to becoming the most famous woman in the world - beautiful, feted, royal and troubled.

In the 'Interactive mode' he'd visited her childhood, felt her anxiety at her parents' constant warring and subsequent separation. He'd seen her transform from a gauche, awkward teenager into a sophisticated young woman, celebrated for her beauty. Saw her marry young, and watched it all go dreadfully wrong. He'd felt her pain over her husband's infidelity, endured her wretchedness over the divorce. But at the same time, he'd seen her use her fame to call attention to causes hitherto ignored. He'd observed how every move of hers created a frenzy, even noted the little details of how her ash-blonde hair changed from a soft, layered do to a short, choppy pixie through various iterations, as though signalling the turbulence and change in her own life.

To every seminal moment of her existence, he'd become the shadow that she could not see. And all along, he'd plotted and planned her death.

He supposed there was a certain bittersweetness to the fact that he was culling her when she seemed to have found another love, another stab at happiness. Her dramas had been played out so publicly, that he envisaged there would undoubtedly be some public mourning too. It would be interesting to watch that after the Fact. After all, altering history must lead to its own kinds of complications. Did the Governing Body have a department that mopped up the messes these thefts left behind? But that did not concern him. His preoccupation lay with the beautiful life he was going to absorb and make his own. He wondered if Mobo would supply him with the files of her passing and its aftermath. It wouldn't hurt to ask, but then again, did he really care?

The evening he had picked was a warm one in August 1997. Whooshing backwards through the Time Tunnel, through years, decades, centuries, it had felt as though only a moment had elapsed. He had picked a visage so plain as to be practically anonymous, camouflaged easily by the humming, throbbing reality of life around him. In the Ponts de Arts where lovers padlocked symbols of their devotion on the railings of its bridge, in the wide avenue of the Champs-Elysées where people strolled arm in arm; in the centuries of art lovingly curated within the Louvre, and in the hauteur of the Tour Eiffel, imposing in her majesty. He slipped through it all, registering all that had changed and all that remained the same.

He had followed her and her companion into the glitzy hotel in central Paris. The meal had taken far too long, and he'd felt nauseous watching them exchange lovesick glances. Finally, they were escorted out of the rear entrance while a decoy vehicle pulled away from the main one. He'd followed their Mercedes a short distance away in his own nondescript white Fiat, allowing the paparazzi to race past him. There was still time.

Just before the entrance of the tunnel, he overtook them, simultaneously triggering the time-release drug in the chauffeur's bloodstream. He'd imperceptibly injected it into him earlier in the day, brushing past the chauffeur on a busy street. Now, it took him instantly over the limit, as though he'd been drinking all evening long; as though his blood was saturated with alcohol. The car gained speed. He saw the startled look on his target's face as his little car passed her sleek ride. He swerved towards them suddenly, causing the chauffeur to veer wildly to the left. That was all it took. The car careened off course, collided head-on with the pillar at a terrible speed, and spun and hit the stone wall of the tunnel backwards, finally coming to a stop.

In the ensuing panic and confusion, he slipped into the crowd of bystanders. He watched her shock and distress with a smug, disembodied ownership; watched as she was pulled out from the wreckage and whisked away to the hospital, knowing in his mind that she didn't have long.

Using the Time Tunnel to return as per Mobo's instructions, Robert couldn't help but wonder how long it would be before she was his to have and to hold.

Back in his bed that night, the voices in his mind seemed louder, more strident, as though cautioning and reprimanding him all at once. He hushed them with a ferocious hostility, secure in the knowledge that once she inhabited him, they would die down forever. He tossed and turned, wondering at what might be happening in her world, wondering how he would hear of his reward.

The message on the ceiling the next morning simply said: *It's done.* Next to it was the figure he'd so eagerly awaited: *Forty-eight years.*

A moment's calm passed over him. He had gained another lifetime.

Then the buzzing started. Whispers upon whispers. Images super-imposed upon images. His head felt like it would explode. His life and hers bumped and crashed into each other, pulverising every coherent thought he held. There was a screaming inside of him, a wail that he could not control, making every nerve-end quiver in pain. His limbs felt heavy, as though he was dragging another weight within them.

With growing horror, he ran out into the street, holding his head, shaking uncontrollably. Those living, thriving thieves of lives looked at him with a distant, knowing condescension. "Welcome to our world," they seemed to say. You've checked in. You. Can. Never. Check. Out.

Now he understood their nervous tics, their dead eyes, and their substance-abuse; their barely-suppressed horror masked, always masked, as gratitude for longevity.

He sank onto his knees, knowing that the consequence of his theft would be another forty-eight years of being trapped in this body, with the life and soul of another held hostage within him. The tsunami of her agony simply drowned out his future.

A long lonely wail began somewhere in the pit of his stomach, rising through his chest, racing past his heart, and swimming up his throat, only to find the doorway of his lips sealed forever.

SWEET DREAMS

Lukas barely suppressed a yawn. He had been coerced into yet another apprenticeship by his overbearing father when all he wanted to do was join the military and travel around Europe.

"Now, make sure this cools at exactly the right temperature. I want the gloss on it preserved, do you understand?"

"Yes master," he replied hastily. It wouldn't do to lose this position as well. He had been careless and willfully incompetent in all the previous ones, much to his employers' chagrin and his father's ire. He'd only been hired at the bakery because of his father's and Wolfgang's long association. But he knew that opportunities were running out just as quickly as his father's patience.

With one last glower, Wolfgang walked out to serve his customers at the front of the bakery. Thus far he had been less than impressed with Lukas and didn't hesitate in displaying his disapproval at any given time.

Lukas set about cooling the chocolate with minimal concentration. His mind was still on the stories Thomas had regaled him with the last time he'd been home - stories of the wine and women, and the beautiful landscapes of Provence. He'd felt so envious, so useless, so tied down, it angered him to even think of it.

"Working hard again, Lukas?" Lena giggled behind him.

He blushed furiously in response. Lena made most men nervous, but on him, her effect was even more exaggerated. He knew she enjoyed teasing him in that flirtatious slant-eyed way of hers. Her bosom seemed to spill out of her corseted top as she leaned over to inspect his handiwork. He felt a sudden stirring as her hand brushed his as she gently took the bowl out of his hands.

"Not like this, you silly boy! Treat the chocolate as you would a lover. Pamper it, cajole it, make it do your bidding."

He watched her in mild surprise. He had no idea she knew so much about chocolate. Her father certainly hadn't taught her. In fact, if Wolfgang saw her here, he would have a colossal fit.

"Lena, I think you should leave. Your father won't approve."

She looked at him and scowled. "When has he ever approved of anything I do? No matter. You carry on with ruining good chocolate."

With a flounce of her skirts, she was gone. Just in time as well. Wolfgang returned with barely suppressed excitement emanating from his normally grouchy person.

"I have news. Big news! The Prince has several important guests visiting in a fortnight. All the chefs in town have been assigned the task of creating the most delectable dessert they possibly could. The winner will not just pocket a 1000 gulden, but might also oust the head chef off his lofty perch. Can you imagine, boy? The glory ... the wealth ..." He sighed in happiness, a dreamy faraway look in his eyes.

Then he looked at Lukas and immediately frowned.

"No more fooling around, do you hear? This is serious business. We need to get started straight away. I must create a torte so exquisite, so divinely delicious that it will leave all competitors trailing. Lukas, I will be famous and rich, if I win. No, no, wipe that look off your face. If you help me create this cake, I will reward you handsomely. I may even give you your freedom ..."

At this, Lukas' ears perked up. He peered at Wolfgang with uncertainty. Was he really being offered freedom?

"Yes, you heard me. A nice little sum of money, and you can be off on your travels. I will intercede with your father. But only," he raised his hand, "if you work hard enough for us to win."

Lukas nodded vigorously, too overwhelmed to say anything.

The next few days went by in a flurry of activity. Wolfgang was forever weighing or measuring or putting down notes in his little black book. Business carried on as usual, but both Lukas and Wolfgang toiled well above their normal hours of work.

A week away from the event though, Wolfgang did not appear in the kitchen. Lukas found him sitting by the fireplace shivering violently.

"I am sick, boy," he announced despondently. The blanket slipped off his shoulders and he doubled up in pain. Lena came in with a hot broth, and spooned it into her father's mouth.

"Lukas, shut the *Konditorei* today. Father is in no condition."

"No!" He shouted, between spasms. "No ... you must carry on as normal. No one must know I am sick. We have to compete ... I cannot fail now ..." He fell back into the chair, exhausted.

Lukas and Lena exchanged looks.

"Yes father, you rest. Lukas can work on the recipe and I can assist him."

At this, Wolfgang scowled with such intensity that he seemed almost well.

"I will not have my daughter parading around the kitchen, and flaunting herself before the customers! Young women from good homes don't put themselves on display in this way, nor do they interfere in men's work! You ... you stay out of his way ...The boy will do it ... He has my notes...." He ran out of breath, leaning back in his chair, exhausted.

Lukas backed out slowly, wondering what on earth he was going to do. Wolfgang was patently too unwell, and Lukas had neither the expertise nor the experience it would take to create this decadent dessert.

The answer came soon enough. Lena entered the kitchen with her apron on, a determined look on her face.

"Before you say anything, Lukas, you and I both know that you are incapable of realising my father's ambition. Whereas I am." She smiled slowly. "He need never know. You can take all the credit, I don't mind."

"Why do it then, Lena? Your father will be livid if he finds out."

"I'm doing it for love," she quipped enigmatically. "Right then, where are father's notes?"

She perused them quickly. Lukas couldn't help but note how lovely she looked. She looked up at him and laughed. "No funny business Lukas! I am the boss's daughter, after all."

Wolfgang had nothing on Lena though. She was a slave driver. Lukas had never felt quite as wrung-out as he did by the end of that day. They had sifted the flour, melted the chocolate, separated the egg whites from the yolks; they had stirred, they had mixed, they had ground. On and on and on they'd gone. All this while, Lukas had dealt with the customers at the shop front as well.

At long last, they were ready to bake the torte.

"Can I ask you something, Lena?"

"Hmmm?"

"There were no ground almonds in your father's recipe?"

"I know," she said quietly, turning her back on him. "Come in early tomorrow to help me ice the torte."

Finally it was done, and it was exquisite. A three-tiered torte beyond compare. The ganache glistened on the surfaces like a polished mirror. Chocolate curlicues formed an arabesque pattern, swirling gently around the torte, almost seeming to embrace this otherworldly confection.

Lukas stood back, awed at what he'd helped create. Never in his life had he seen something quite so seductively tantalising.

"You are a genius!" He exclaimed.

"No, *you* are the genius. Don't forget, I have done nothing to help you."

Wolfgang had been improving steadily, and had started to notice

Lena's absences. On the day before the public unveiling of the competitors' creations he hobbled into the kitchen.

"Well? Where is it? What are you putting out in front of the Prince, in my name? I tell you now boy, if it is not good enough, we are not entering the competition. I do not want to lose the few loyal customers I have."

Lukas led him to the torte. It stood in a cool corner of the kitchen, serenely magnificent. Wolfgang stopped in his tracks. He seemed to be lost for words. He circled the creation, leaned forward to sniff it, and then stood back quickly, almost hitting his head on the low ceiling.

"You did this? From my recipe?"

Lukas nodded.

"I see." Wolfgang looked at him. "Well then, it seems I have grossly underestimated your talents. I will be happy for this to be entered in my name."

The next day, the square was buzzing with excitement. The Prince was due to arrive at any moment. Fanciful creations jostled with plainer counterparts while the chefs stood by, eying each other's handiwork with envy or disdain. Wolfgang and Lukas stood quietly by their own torte. It didn't scream or shout out in garish colours. It reached out in a muted whisper: to entice, to tantalise.

The Prince stood by it, quite enchanted. A man of slender proportions, his penchant for desserts was only revealed in the beginnings of a belly, tightly cinched under a thin leather belt embroidered with colourful flowers. Dressed in pale blue, his red brocade waistcoat stood out in stark contrast to the drab colours worn by the townspeople. His entourage was similarly dressed in rich purples and greens. Wolfgang and Lukas looked at him in awe. His long and pointy beard quivered with anticipation. "May I?" He asked, reaching for a fork. A look of pure ecstasy passed over his face as he tasted the first mouthful. He closed his eyes, allowing himself to savour the flavours of the torte. Then he looked at Wolfgang briefly before reaching out for another forkful, then another and another. A murmur ran through the crowd.

.   .   .

Back at the *Konditorei*, Lena lingered by the window in apprehension. Wolfgang had been categorical in his refusal to allow her to accompany him, but there had been an odd look in his eyes and he had kissed her cheek absently when she had wished him luck. She knew how much this day meant to him and she hoped that her torte would not disappoint, even if it didn't win. As she saw a lone familiar figure making its way home on their horse and cart, she rushed downstairs.

"Father!" Lena ran up to Wolfgang, concerned. "Where is Lukas? What happened? Why are you alone?"

"Lukas is gone." He sat down heavily. "We won."

A bemused look came over his face and he beckoned her to him. He held Lena's hands in his own, turning them over, examining her long delicate fingers. Then he pulled her down until she kneeled in front of him. Gently, he moved a lock of hair off her face.

"Well, my beautiful, talented girl. Are you ready to do it all over again for the Prince's guests?"

Lena smiled with pure happiness and buried her face in her father's chest.

STALKER

The bins are heavy as I drag them outside. It's a blustery day and my scarf is struggling to escape off my head. The sunglasses keep sliding down my nose, and I push them back impatiently. The disguise must remain. Even if it's only 6 a.m. and no one is on the street yet, the disguise must remain. I place the bins side-by-side, like two upright soldiers called to attention, one black and one blue. Rubbish and recycling. I have gone through everything painstakingly, shredded every last document so that no traces of me remain in there.

I hobble back indoors, bent over slightly. My back has been playing up again and maybe it's time to go back to physio, except that I can't bear to be touched or examined, even by that gentle Indian doctor. So I will take the painkillers and soldier on. Ah! I smile to myself. The girl may leave the army, but the army never leaves the girl.

After I eat my Weetabix in the conservatory, surrounded by my wonderful green garden with its apple trees and flowering wisteria, I pull out the laptop.

Facebook. This nameless, faceless existence I have chosen for myself is at once obliterated.

There I am, in full technicolour on my fan page. Blonde hair flying, lips in a red pout. Gold lycra clinging to every curve. In my heyday, I was the most famous woman on the planet, and they will not let me forget it. Why did I agree to get hooked up to this infernal thing? Gert had thought it would be a distraction. Did he *want* to remind me of the good old days, in the hopes that I might want to revive my career? Well, if anything, it makes my present course seem like the most sensible thing I have ever done. I was never good at handling the kind of intrusion that fame inevitably brought into my life, and fame poked and prodded at me until wounded, I'd retreated so far away that no one could reach me.

Then why do I compulsively check this page every day, reading the good things and the bad? I look at all the pictures and chuckle over the comments my many fans put on here. Gert had said it would make them feel connected to me, that it would be a place they could meet and discuss my work, and rhapsodise about my music.

Now, that life seems like a million years ago and I am happy to leave it that way. I want to be a bystander to the circus.

I scroll down the page to see what else has been added - old songs, photos, memories of people who saw me in concerts, messages pleadingly asking me to make a comeback. Then I see it. A message in my inbox. It's him again.

Hello? Katja it's me. Please answer. Why do you persist in ignoring me?

———

Looking back, the ascent to the top was really easy. Too easy. I got the recognition I'd craved for my music so fast that I hadn't known what to do with it. It had scared me even back then.

As a child, I was an inveterate performer. It did not take much persuasion from my parents to stand in front of a room full of guests and belt out a number. I basked in the glow of being admired, welcoming the compliments as my due. Then teenhood happened and I retreated. In the sanctuary that was my room, I hid from the world and the incessant arguments between my soon-to-be-divorced parents.

In the wilderness of those years, music was my only companion. Even when, seeking order and discipline, I signed up to the army as a direct rebellion to my mother's party lifestyle, I never abandoned my first love.

Every evening at the army camp, I would entertain my mates with a medley of self-composed songs. It was on one such evening, as I hummed and strummed, that a mate suggested that I was perhaps better suited to being in the spotlight on stage, rather than on the frontline. I agreed, as the daily grind of military life had long lost its allure. She put me in touch with her uncle who knew a record producer, and before I knew it, my amateurish tape of home-produced songs was winging its way to him.

The rest was a blur of performances, awards and fame. Too much fame.

———

You know I will find you. I always do. You are my one true love. If only you would give us a chance.

My hand shakes as I pour myself a cup of tea. How could he possibly know that I check this page from my fake account? After all, the page could have been set up by anyone. Is he hazarding a guess? This is the third house I have moved to in the last five years. Each time I look over my shoulder, his shadowy presence threatens my every move. Gert thinks I am being paranoid. I have never actually encountered the man, but I feel him there - his eyes upon me, watching, waiting to strike.

I punch in the number quickly. It rings for a while before Gert answers.

"Katja."

"I'm scared, Gert."

"What now?" He sounds sleepy and exasperated.

"He's found me again."

"Who has?"

"The stalker."

"That's impossible, Katja. You know we've taken every precaution. There is no way on earth he could have found you. I am the only one who knows where you are."

"He's sending me messages on Facebook."

"On your private account?"

"No, on the public one ... the fan page one."

I can hear him breathe deeply before he responds. "Listen Katja, there are a lot of weirdos and nutters out there. People write all sorts of things on Facebook. It's an open forum. It doesn't mean he's targeting you. Hell, it may not even be him!"

"I know it's him," I insist.

"Like the time you were certain he was hiding in the rose bush, or when you thought he was pretending to be the postman?"

"I know you think I am a silly old woman. But he's pursued me for so many years, and I can tell it's him again. He calls himself KL. Just that. He's using an old photo of mine as his profile picture, and it has a heart with a dagger superimposed on it."

"It's only Facebook. Don't respond. He can't know you've read it - for all he knows, it could be your assistant handling that side of things."

"B ... but what if he finds me again? What if he knows where I'm living?"

I can hear Gert's sigh.

"Ok, fine. What do you want to do? Move again? That can be arranged."

———

The thing is that I have grown to love this house. I feel like I'm finally growing roots. I am not a part of the community yet, it is too early for that. But this bungalow feels like home, and I don't want to move. So I've decided to ignore this nagging feeling and stay off Facebook for a while.

There are some beautiful nature walks near where I live and I intend to make full use of them. The delayed onset of summer weather means that I can cover-up, and with my hat and sunglasses on, I look no different from the multitude of middle-aged women walking around the lake in the morning.

The lake is like a placid sheet of glass and I watch the few ripples that a lonely swan creates behind him. The dog walkers, the yummy mummies, the serious joggers and the semi-serious cyclists are all out in full force. It's turning into a glorious day, and loath as I am, I pull off my hat and scarf. It's just too warm to keep them on and no one has displayed an iota of curiosity towards the middle-aged woman ambling slowly amongst them. I feel buoyant in anonymity. Perhaps there is hope after all.

Your hair is like spun gold, did you know? Even with the few streaks of grey in there. You looked beautiful this morning, my love. Fresh air and exercise are doing you good.

I slam the laptop shut, my heart thudding. He's found me. How? HOW?

It takes a while for my shaking to subside. Then I retrieve the shoebox from under the bed, and slowly remove the lid. In there lies twenty-five years of obsession. Letters written in blood, Valentine cards that spelt out in gory detail all that he would do to me once I was his. Everything signed KL. Katja's Love.

Gert had always wanted to turn it over to the police. I hadn't. At first, because I laughed it off. And then because it was a constant reminder of why I'd had to leave that life behind.

Once again I ring up Gert.

"I think it's time to tell the police."

My case officer is a pleasant young woman called Hillary. She is too young to register quite how big a star I was. She peers at me uncertainly.

"Miss Nilsson, why have you never spoken of this before?"

"I felt that if I somehow melted away ... disappeared ... he would too."

"But he didn't. I find it curious that he locates you each time. Do you think your manager, this Gert Peeters, could be letting things slip?"

"Gert isn't just my manager, he is also my nephew. My cousin's son. He's family, and he knows how much I value my privacy."

She looks doubtful but nods her head and shuts the file in front of her.

"There is not a lot we can do till he contacts you again. We'll be monitoring the Facebook page for any further messages. It's a shame you deleted the old ones, we could have had a clue to work with. Why did you delete them again?" She peers at me as I mumble my response, still in a daze. "You panicked? Yes, well ... Anyhow, if he sends another message, it will be fairly easy to trace the IP address, and through that get a fix on his location. Please take your usual precautions, but live your life normally."

I nearly laugh at that. Normalcy was never an option.

———

Weeks have gone by without any messages. I can tell that Hillary is disinterested by now, putting it down to an over fertile imagination.

I am, in part relieved, but anxious too. I know that as soon as the surveillance is removed, he will be back. I hope he gets impatient before then. I need someone to believe me and right now the chances are looking grim. I go about my daily business, which really just amounts to a morning walk, watching some daytime television, making myself lunch, trawling through Facebook, and then cooking myself dinner. It is a lonely existence, and the spare room full of my music memorabilia is a testament to how far I have wandered off my original path. Why couldn't I have been left to do what I wanted to? Perform and melt away, rejuvenate and then return to perform again. Why did fame have to become this threat to my safety, my privacy, occupying far too much space in my life and my mind? To this day, the memories chafe like the serrated edges of a rusty blade.

Sometimes, when I'm in a nostalgic mood, I strum my guitar and try to sing a few lines. But then I collapse into sobs. There is no way back. No, none at all.

———

The neighbour's cat is a mangled mess on my doorstep. The blood-smeared message says 'BITCH'.

Hillary keeps making cups of tea for me, while the other officers take samples and clean up.

"Has he ever gotten this close before?"

"No ... never. I've suspected that he's nearby, but this ... this ..."

I can't stop trembling. This kind of violence is new. He is getting desperate, and I am desperately scared.

"We've posted an officer to watch over you. Don't worry, Miss Nilsson. We'll be around. He won't be able to come anywhere near you."

———

The Press is swarming out there. All those years of hiding, and now they have found me.

'RECLUSIVE KATJA DISCOVERED IN SURREY HIDE HOLE', scream the headlines.

Gert is doing damage control from New York. I feel suffocated, claustrophobic, paranoid. I cannot even sit out in my garden for fear that the long lens cameras will capture more candid shots.

'FAT AND UGLY - WHAT HAPPENED TO KATJA?'

I examine myself in the mirror. Am I really that fat and ugly? A frumpish woman scowls back at me, lending credence to the screeching tabloids. When did this happen?

"You need to give an interview," Gert commands.

"No ... I can't. Don't ask this of me, Gert. You know how much I hate all this."

"Katja, satisfy their curiosity and they'll back off. But if you keep up the Garbo act, they will hound you to your grave!"

"What about him?"

"Who?" asks Gert impatiently.

"The stalker! KL! I don't want him to know any more about me. Any more than he's already found out."

"Oh, Auntie!"

Gert only calls me Auntie when he feels sorry for me.

"The police are on it. And with the Press around, he won't be able to get a look-see. They'll nab him soon enough. I told you, you should've gone to them ages ago."

Suddenly I am exhausted from the hiding, the running, the fending off of people.

"Okay, I'll do it."

———

He sits across from me, this young reporter with the piercing blue eyes. I've already forgotten his name, and am too embarrassed to ask again.

"So, Miss Nilsson, may I call you Katja?" I nod in assent. "I must say at the outset, what a huge fan I am." He seems too young to know my music. "I had a big poster of you in my bedroom as a teenager. I think you might have been every red-blooded male's fantasy back then."

I flush. I should be flattered, but instead I feel uncomfortable. This was the sort of attention I had sought to escape. I'm old enough to be his mother. I don't *want* to be spawning fantasies.

"Why did you, at the peak of your career, decide to retire?"

The well-rehearsed answer sits on the tip of my tongue. The change of musical tastes, the evolution of the industry, the mass-produced pop stars - everything Gert has made me practice over and over.

"I was tired," I say.

"Tired of what? The music?"

"The fame game."

"It was voluntary? This withdrawal from the public eye?"

"Yes, yes it was."

He leans back on the chair and smiles. His teeth are white and even, and I think then that he resembles a shark.

"So, nothing to do with the nodules that were discovered on your vocal cords then?"

I stiffen. Sensing my unease, he leans in for the kill.

"That must've been so difficult for you. Discovering that you wouldn't be able to sing those high notes anymore?"

When I don't answer, he abruptly switches tack.

"I hear you are being stalked?"

Nowhere in Gert's brief with this particular newspaper were either of these points mentioned. This was meant to be a gentle reintroduction to the world, not a public mauling.

Twenty years ago I would have stood up and walked out, imperious and diva-like. Now I sit here like a deer caught in the headlights. For one thing, I have nowhere to go. This is my home. Secondly, I am unused to throwing my weight about anymore. I size him up and then give him a tremulous smile.

"Yes, it's true that I cannot sing the way I once did, but that does not mean I can't write either. As you know, I wrote all my own songs. I could have still had a career had I wanted one. I just chose not to. As for being stalked, there are any number of strange people who fixate on celebrities for the lack of something in their own lives. Giving them undue importance is just that."

Satisfied, I take a sip of my tea, a slight smile playing around my lips.

"Yet this is not just a run-of-the-mill obsessive fan, is it? He's a long term stalker. Someone who's been leaving you little presents lately."

I exhale sharply. This man is too well informed and his source must lie within the force.

"I really do not wish to speak about it. This is a police matter now, and I suggest we leave it with them."

———

I am not surprised to read a less than flattering piece on me in the newspaper. He describes me as an ageing prima donna with delusions of grandeur. I laugh and throw it aside. So much for speaking aloud! Now perhaps they will leave me in peace.

Some do and some don't. The press has had its fill. The public isn't that interested to discover that behind all those mysterious years lies another spent talent. It's the music producers who start sending the feelers.

"Katja, I've been receiving so many phone calls from people who thought you'd fallen off the face of the planet!" Gert shouts excitedly down the phone. "They want you to write for them, for the new singers. Come on, isn't it time? Why are you burying yourself in some Godforsaken village? You have more talent in that little finger of yours than most of these young ones do in their entire bodies!"

I grimace at that. Gert is prone to hyperbole when he gets fired up. Although it does get me thinking. What's stopping me now?

———

My second lease on this career is going so well that I have forgotten all about KL. Till he resurfaces.

This time it's a bunch of roses outside my front door. A bouquet of white with a solitary crimson rose. I start shaking. I look around furtively and then pick up the bouquet. A note falls out.

My girl is writing again. Such lovely songs. Are they for me?

Hillary arrives three hours later, by which time I've worked myself into a state. I'm pacing up and down. My hair is a mess, and she takes a step back at the crazed look in my eyes.

"Calm down, Miss Nilsson. This has arrived how many months later? Four, five? We'll send the note to the lab for analysis, but I really think he might be losing steam."

I look at her incredulously. "Losing steam? The note is written in blood! This man will never let go of me. What are you doing about it? When are you going to catch him?"

"We don't have a lot to go on. I posted a few plainclothes men here a few times and they spotted no suspicious characters. Whoever he is, he covers his tracks well. So well to almost be a phantom, Miss Nilsson."

"One you're supposed to find! How will I ever feel safe while he's out there?"

I break down then. Sobs wrack my body while she pats me on the shoulder and mutters something soothing.

———

There is a cool breeze and I pull the covers up to my chin, trying to remember if I've left the window open. My feet feel cold, and I rub them together. There is a distant sound of music and laughter. A party, I think sleepily.

Suddenly I'm wide awake, my heart thumping. He's in the room. I can sense him. I reach for the steak knife I keep under my pillow but it isn't there. I panic, and squeeze my eyes shut, hoping he hasn't noticed my laboured breathing. His hand reaches under the covers and touches my leg.

I wake up screaming.

I look around the room frantically. There is no one. It's the nightmare, the same one I've had since I was fourteen. Since Mama's first boyfriend after the divorce decided he wanted to play with me instead of her.

He was the first of many. Till I finally escaped to the army. Yet the ghost of him lingers in every nook and cranny of my life.

———

I start looking for houses. Somewhere even more remote and rural. If I have to run all my life, I'm going to make it as difficult as possible for him to follow me.

Gert rings me on a Sunday morning.

"Katja, there is a favour I have to ask of you."

"What is it?" I am wary. I don't like giving or receiving favours.

"It's Papa's 70th Birthday. We're having a big party. The whole family will be there. I'd like you to come."

The whole family. I haven't seen them in years. Not since that spectacular falling out after which I severed ties with all except Gert.

"It's time to make your peace, Auntie. This is the perfect occasion to do it. Everyone will be there. It can be like the old times again. Please say you'll come. I'll book the flights and the hotel immediately if you do."

I find myself agreeing reluctantly.

———

Five days later I am boarding a flight to New York. It's been years since I was surrounded by as many impatient people, pushing and shoving and getting irritated with my slow-moving ways. I'm confused at the airport, with the new regulations of having to put liquids in plastic bags and walk through metal detectors shoeless. I'm confused with the flight numbers and the gates, with the Duty-Free shops filled with perfumes, alcohol and chocolates. I am confused and I am scared. The world has changed a lot since I became a hermit.

The flight is uneventful, and the overweight American man I sit next to snores the entire way. I try to concentrate on the film on my personal monitor, but my thoughts flit here and there, a jumble of memories and conversations, of accusations and anger.

A flight attendant walks by me, then stops. She kneels in front and I brace myself for the usual gushing.

"Are you okay? You look rather pale. Would you like some water?"

I nod gratefully. I needn't have bothered with all that camouflage over the years. My body is its own disguise.

———

The car whisks me to a Manhattan hotel. Gert has spared no expense. He's clearly done well out of my royalties. I snooze on the King size bed, dreading the evening's get-together. The party is scheduled for tomorrow, but tonight is about getting reacquainted.

I dress carefully in the black dress I bought online. Even at size eighteen, it clings to every lump and bump of my misshapen figure. I apply some red lipstick that must at least be a few decades old. It smells off, just like I do. The phone rings just as I am spritzing on some perfume. It's Gert. He's waiting in the lobby.

We walk into his Penthouse apartment, arm in arm. Gert is tall and handsome with his salt and pepper hair, and I am short and stout and visibly nervous.

They all come and greet me silently, a kiss on each cheek. Mama sits proudly in her wheelchair, ever the matriarch, waiting for me to go to her. I do. I kneel down and kiss her proffered cheek.

"The prodigal daughter returns," she notes dryly, her breath a mix of whiskey and cigarettes, her voice as husky as I remember it.

I smile and move towards Gert's father. He greets me stiffly, still not forgiving the last fracas. Families! I sigh inwardly and keep smiling.

Wine loosens tongues and over time the awkwardness dissipates. I stick to soda water and don't add much to the conversation. I have nothing to add anyhow. Talk is about the extended family who I haven't been in touch with, current affairs that I have no clue of, and people who have died, whose funerals I did not attend.

It's strange how disconnected I feel from these people. They are my blood but somehow, I have never belonged. Always an outsider, the only reason they ever tolerated me was because I was famous. Then, like a trophy that had lost its sheen, I was set aside and forgotten. Funny how these people know so little about me and care even less. Then there is KL, who by his very obsessiveness cares too much. So much that he petrifies me.

I sip on my soda water, wondering how long before I can politely take my leave.

"Katja, are you taking your medicines?" I turn around, startled. Mama is smirking up at me. "Are you? You know it's the only way to control your condition."

Everybody turns to look, eyes staring at me: questioning, judging.

Gert comes and lays a hand on her shoulder to hush her up. I turn and stumble out of the room. This was a bad idea, a very bad idea indeed.

———

I wake up with a thumping headache and a hollow feeling in the pit of my stomach. Last night I got very, very drunk after a very long time. I'm not sure what I said or did but I do remember the look of horror on Gert's face. I remember him dragging me out and putting me to bed. I sit up, and the room spins around me. With a groan, I fall back upon the pillow. Mama's face swims into my mind, shock and disgust writ large on it.

Nausea hits me suddenly and I stagger to the bathroom and throw up in the toilet. Shaking, I move towards the basin to wash my face.

You naughty, naughty girl.

My red lipstick lies abandoned on the side, the script on the mirror screaming its message out to me silently. Aghast, I back away.

I walk the streets of Manhattan for hours. At one point I find myself on a bench in Central Park, as a horse-drawn carriage with a young couple goes by. There is a surreal quality to this morning. I feel everything is too vivid; the colours too loud, the sunshine too bright. The cacophony of the traffic is assaulting my eardrums, but I walk on, uncaring, unseeing.

The sun is setting as I wander back into the hotel lobby. The manager approaches me.

"Miss Nilsson, there have been several messages for you. Mr Peeters came to pick you up around noon, but there was no response from your room. We, uh, had to enter to check that you were okay. The room has been cleaned. Is there anything I can get you?"

I walk past him blindly.

There is a note on the dresser. It's from Gert: 'Come if you can.'

But I can't.

I flick through the Television channels, unable to comprehend anything. Finally, succumbing to the gnawing in my stomach I order dinner. And a double vodka.

KATJA NILSSON FOUND DEAD IN NEW YORK HOTEL ROOM

In what appears to be a suicide, Miss Nilsson, yesteryear superstar was found dead in the bathtub of her Manhattan hotel room. She had recently emerged from a self-imposed exile. However, reports indicate that her mental state was extremely fragile. It appears that whilst Miss Nilsson claimed that she was the victim of a stalker, she was, in fact, suffering from paranoid schizophrenia. Her family had long urged for medical and psychiatric intervention that she had refused, choosing instead to barricade herself from the world. Her nephew and manager had this official statement to make: 'It is with great sadness that we bid Katja goodbye. She lives on in our hearts through her extraordinary music, the legacy of a tragic and troubled life. Kindly leave us to mourn her in peace.'

The grave headstone reads:

Here lies Katja Liv Nilsson. Born September 4, 1955, Died August 18, 2011.

KL Nilsson. Adored by the world, loved only by herself.

MAYBE

Last night I dreamt of Fairfield again. The mist was swirling around the house, shrouding it, trying to reach its wraithlike tentacles inside. I sensed the figure near my bed, its loathing lashing at me in waves. I tried to speak, to explain, but it reached out and covered my face with a pillow. I could not breathe ... I could not breathe ... There was smoke all around me and I crawled to try and reach the front door, but something held me back ... my legs would not move ... they were caught in a vice-like grip ... I knew then that I was going to die ...

I sit upright in the bed, my heart thudding wildly, rivulets of sweat streaming down my face. My legs are entangled in the sheets. Pale light has begun to creep in through the curtains and I look to my right, but Max isn't there. I find him sitting on the porch, as I usually do these mornings. He is smoking. From the stubs I can tell that he has been there a while. I go up behind him, and my slender arms encase his shoulders. He turns and lets me kiss his cheek. The puckered skin is smooth to the touch and once again, I feel a lurch to see my handsome husband's face so marred by hatred and jealousy.

"Should we go to the beach today?" I ask him.

"It's too hot. Maybe another day. I'll work on the novel. You carry on ..."

Stepping back inside, my worries resurface. The distance between us seems to be increasing. He carries his guilt around like a cross. Nothing I say or do seems to lighten that burden. I slip out of my shorts and T-shirt and stand under the cool shower. Tears run down my face, mingling with the water, washing my sorrow down the drain and into the sea, to lap at a different shore. I don't hear him come in. Then suddenly, he is behind me and I turn and offer myself to him. We make love, and once again, I feel connected. I feel whole.

It was the start of the dry season, the month of May. The cafés were getting busy again, and in the usual scrum of tourists, he seemed to stand apart. It wasn't just the crisp white shirt and khakis he wore almost every day. It was his demeanour. He almost seemed to be sleepwalking. As though life had clubbed him around the head, and he no longer knew or cared where he was. Every day he would sit at the same table, drink the same coffee and smoke the same cigarettes, staring out into the horizon. Every day he would leave me a tip of Rp 50,000 - a princely sum. After the third day, I tried to refuse the tip.

"Please sir, it is not necessary. It is too much. It is my job to serve you. I cannot accept ..."

His eyes seemed to register me for the first time.

"No, please. Take it."

And he thrust the money into my hand and walked out.

Afterwards, we sit and eat breakfast together. Our conversation is limited to what I need to buy from the shops.

"I need some more biros. The ink seems to dry up quickly in this hot weather."

"Max?"

"Yes?"

"Why don't you use the laptop? Writing longhand must be tiring for you. I can always get Wayan to fix the connection."

He pushes his plate away, his toast half-eaten.

"I prefer writing this way, Dayu."

Then he is on the porch again, smoking. The pages of his spiral notebook blowing back and forth between the covers, sparse lines etched carelessly within.

When he first leaned over and kissed me, the breath seemed to leave my body for a long long time. How deeply I was in love with this man I had scarcely known for two months.

"Marry me."

"A Bule?" My mother was shocked. "You cannot marry this white man! And go and live in his cold country? They are all made of ice, these foreigners. He wants to take you back as a maid. Dayu, I cannot permit this."

Permit she did in the end, albeit reluctantly. I was glad to have her blessings. She was the only immediate family I had, and she too died while I was abroad.

I cycle to the shop in Ubud. A distant cousin of my mother owns it. Ketut sits there all day, toothlessly grinning at all the young women who come in. They don't seem to mind. It is a pleasant way to while away the time, although I wonder how he makes any money from the jumble of items he stocks in there.

"More biros? Does that husband of yours do anything at all, but let the ink run dry on these?"

I smile and wander to the back of the store. An old copy of a British Society magazine falls on the floor. I pick it up and casually flick through the pages. There, in full vibrant colour, I come upon her picture. My hands start trembling but I can't stop staring at that perfectly chiselled face: that cruel mocking smile, those eyes that seem to bore into me, stripping me of all my secrets, denying me of my existence. The world goes dark quite suddenly.

He never promised it would be easy. And it wasn't. His sudden black moods. The long journey to his country from mine. I stood and shivered in the greyness of it all. His chauffeur was late. I looked around to see people rushing past. No one smiled. No one exchanged glances.

"Heathrow is one of the busiest airports in the world," he reassured me. "This is quite normal. Once we're in the countryside, you won't feel so out of place."

I wondered at that. Bali was a pleasant and welcoming place. It greeted you with genuine warmth. Here I felt lost and alien, my mind and body unable to comprehend the change.

He was silent the entire car journey and my tired eyes drooped as the grey buildings gave way to what he called a motorway, and then to greener vistas. I must have fallen asleep for I felt him shaking me awake gently.

"Dayu, my beautiful one, we're here. This is home."

My sharp intake of breath made him grimace. His 'country pile' was enormous. He had never told me, never described the wealth he came from. Our tiny home in Bali would have fit into one of his living rooms.

"I did nothing to earn this. We inherited it. It costs an arm and a leg to maintain. I wish I could get rid of it. Especially after ..." He stopped abruptly.

There were so many gaps, so many blanks in his story that I wanted him to fill. He wouldn't, and I was too afraid to ask. The one thing I did know was that he had a twin sister. A disabled twin who lived in this grand house, and from whom I was to receive a very frosty reception.

I come to my senses on the floor of the shop. Ketut has rolled up some old material and placed it under my head. He sits there watching me, wordlessly chewing on his tobacco.

"I'm sorry!" I exclaim, sitting up. My head swims once again, and I lie back down.

"What happened there, child? Why did you return all fearful, and your husband like ... that?" He waves his hand all over his face, referring to Max's burns.

I curl myself into a foetal position and start to sob. I miss my mother. I miss the innocence of the days gone by. He lets me cry, and once I am done, he brings me some water and waits.

"*Bapak* Ketut, I cannot repeat what I saw. But we came away because we had to. It was the only way to survive."

He's holding the magazine open on the page of her picture. She looks out of the page, her hauteur adding to her ethereal beauty.

"So, who is this then? This woman that made you faint?"

"She's his ex-wife."

The house was a shrine to her. Not a thing had changed since she died. From the furnishings to the photos of them as a couple, as a family, with friends, with her dogs - everything was intact.

"You have to understand, Dayu. Amelia and Becca were childhood friends. Becca still hasn't come to terms with her death."

The elusive Becca had yet to emerge. I dreaded the meeting, especially after our phone conversation, which had been stilted at best. How would she respond to me? Would she view me as the interloper that I was, replacing her beloved sister-in-law and friend in her brother's life and bed?

"So this is the little Balinese doll you picked up on your travels, Max?" She smiled at me coolly. Her wheelchair had made no noise as she'd snuck up on us. Was it my imagination, or was it a deliberate ploy to wrong-foot me, to catch me unawares?

I smiled back at her, leaning down to embrace her. She moved her wheelchair sideways.

"Not so soon, Dayu. That's your name, isn't it? We need to get to know one another. Then you may kiss me."

Hurt, I stepped back.

Max laughed and pulled me close.

"Don't mind Becca. She's as prickly as a hedgehog."

The tea Ketut brings me is sickly sweet. It is just what I need. I sip at it, letting it calm me, feeling the strength returning to my bones.

"She died a couple of years ago," I speak slowly at first, and then the words come out in a gush. "That's when Max came here. He wanted to get away. You see Ketut, she disappeared for a very long time. Then they found her body."

"Murder?"

"Suicide."

He bows his head, thinking. "Was it because of him?"

"No," I say. "Well yes, in a way ... it's so complicated."

"Then tell me, child. You cannot bottle this up forever. It is not healthy. I see what it is doing to you."

I shiver in the heat, and he hurriedly fetches me a shawl to cover myself.

The staff in the house had dwindled to two - a cleaner and a gardener. It took me a few days but I started to see how the house was slowly falling into disrepair and ruin. Neither brother nor sister seemed too bothered with its upkeep. I tried and failed to make it appear homely. It was too large, too grand for that. So we stayed confined to the few habitable rooms there were.

"This is your first Christmas tree, isn't it, my darling?"

Max could sense my excitement as I hung another silver bauble off a branch. With a fire roaring, the cards sitting on the mantelpiece, and the Christmas tree he had helped me put up, I was finally starting to feel like a part of this house.

"Heaven knows she'll get it all wrong! Amelia's trees were always stunningly beautiful. Remember the time they were featured in Perfect Home magazine?"

Max glared at Becca but said nothing. All at once, I felt deflated. Becca never passed up an opportunity to make me feel inferior to my predecessor. And Max never defended me.

"They had known each other all their lives. Their parents were friends. They belonged to the upper crust of society where you only married one of your own."

Ketut nods in understanding. "Go on."

"The sad thing was realising that they didn't love one another after all."

"Then why not divorce? It is acceptable in white society, no?"

"They wanted to but Max's mother fell ill, and then Becca had the accident. Then too much time went by. Oh, it's all too confusing ... I don't know why they stayed married. But they did."

"And they were unhappy?"

"Yes. Max says they were terribly unhappy. He started to travel more for work. She began to have affairs that she didn't bother hiding. The only person that truly bound them together was Becca."

"The sister?"

"Yes, the twin. She was in a wheelchair after the accident and living with them. They both adored her. She was like an extension of them. Breaking up with each other would have meant breaking that bond too."

"You're not half the woman she was!" Becca sneered at me.

Max was out of the country again, and I took to spending my days outside, as far away from his venomous sister as I could. It was clear to me that I would never win her over. No overtures of friendship, no home-cooked meals, no head massages or offers to play Monopoly would ever fill that gaping wound she carried around her like a badge. The loss of her confidante, her friend, her sister.

"Can we not make peace Becca? I do not want to quarrel with you. For Max's sake, please?"

It was getting unbearable. She barely disguised her contempt for me or her hero-worship of Amelia.

"Why did she kill herself? The wife? If she was that beautiful, that talented, that rich?" Ketut enquires.

"Guilt."

"What sort of guilt?"

A wave of nausea assails me then and I shakily make my way to the ramshackle toilet at the back. I retch into the bowl, then splash my face with water, feeling hot and cold alternately.

I had come upon the diary by accident during my irregular cleaning forays. I started reading it out of boredom, and then with the ensuing knowledge that it belonged to Amelia. The entries were commonplace, to begin with. Hairdresser appointments, fittings at boutiques, dog grooming sessions. Then, almost as though she wanted to spill her most intimate thoughts to me, they became more explicit. Assignations with lovers. Details of what they had done. How long the conquests had lasted before she became bored and moved on. I devoured it all with a ghoulish fascination.

Then the entry that shook my world.

"Dayu, you are aware, aren't you?" Ketut asks me gently, handing me a towel.

Shakily I accept. I look at him wonderingly, as he places a wrinkled hand on my stomach and pats it briefly.

"Oh!" I gasp, the age-old knowledge filling me with a strange happiness.

"Perhaps you have said enough for one day. This is not the moment to live in the past. This is the time to celebrate the future. Go on home child."

He ushers me out tenderly.

"It was because of you." I stood before Becca, holding up the diary as proof of my accusation.

She narrowed her eyes, still not following.

"You loved her. But not as a sister. You wanted her for yourself. You could just about share her with Max. But no one else. You drove yourself mad with jealousy over her affairs!"

She laughed then.

"Yes. Yes, I did. She was all I had ever wanted. All my life, I had wanted to possess her. Max had her and he didn't care."

"So you seduced her."

"It was only a few times but it was sublime. It was how it should have been."

"Except she didn't think so. She wanted out."

"Is that her diary you've been reading, you dirty little spy?"

"Did you blackmail her? Is that what you did? Did you threaten to expose her to everyone, to bring down her perfect facade? Did you drive her to her suicide?"

"Shut up! Shut up!!" She screamed at me, wheeling her chair around in fury. "No one will ever understand. No one!"

I stood there suddenly emptied of all rage. The diary dropped out of my hand. I made my way up to bed.

I cycle back slowly, the biros jangling together in the plastic bag that hangs off the handlebar. I've always wondered if Max read the diary when he returned unexpectedly that night, or whether Becca had already set fire to it by then, starting the blaze that would destroy their home. I hope he didn't. What he saw has filled him with enough horror for a lifetime.

The mist was swirling around the house, shrouding it, trying to reach its wraithlike tentacles inside. I sensed the figure near my bed, its loathing lashing at me in waves. I tried to speak, to explain, but it reached out and covered my face with a pillow. I could not breathe ... I could not breathe ...

Her arms had a superhuman amount of strength as she tried to suffocate me. I struggled vainly, my feet kicking out, until they connected with flesh. I heard her grunt of pain and the brief respite was all I needed to wriggle out of bed and crawl towards the door, gasping in lungfuls of air.

Somewhere I could smell smoke. Was something on fire? But uppermost on my mind was escape. I could hear the whirring of her wheels not far behind me, and I sent up a desperate prayer. "Save me ... Oh God, please save me ..."

She threw herself upon me. Her arms were a vice around my legs. Then Max's voice, "Bloody hell Becca ... what are you doing?!"

He tried to save us both. He went back inside the burning house for her. His seared face was a legacy of that futile attempt. Nothing would assuage the guilt of his failure.

I stop to pluck a *Jepun* flower. Frangipani. They are in bloom everywhere. A riot of colours that sings out a summer song. I place it in my hair.

It is the month of May again. It was May, a year ago, when I first met him. A year in which I have learned so much about love and hate, about secrets and buried passions. If I could go back in time, would I choose to marry Max again? I look around me, at the verdant fertile ground of my birthplace and know that I would. I get back on my bicycle, cycling slowly as memories press down upon me. Then I recall Ketut's hand on my stomach and smile.

Perhaps, just perhaps, we could begin afresh. Maybe we could start our story from this point, erasing all the hatred, guilt and wrongdoing, and replacing it with hope and happiness. With a growing certainty, I pedal home faster. To my husband, to my love, and to a future I will not allow to be blighted by the past.

(A tribute to Daphne Du Maurier's 'Rebecca')

HUGE

It's sitting there innocuously, that delicious piece of confectionery. Dark molten chocolate encased in a crackling shell of praline loveliness.

It's sitting there tantalising me with its smoothness, its *roundness,* its sheer perfection. All it would take would be a little stretch of the arm and within no time, it would be in my mouth, melting all of its lusciousness within.

Yet, I'm sitting here glaring at it. Knowing that *this* piece and all the contents of *that* box that arrived anonymously are pure sabotage. No sugar has crossed these lips in three months. All it would take is *one* bite, just a teensy weensy one and it is a slippery slope, my friend.

It wasn't always this way. There was a time when it was effortless. When my boobs bounced as I walked, emphasising my tiny waist. A time when the men whistled at my ass. Hell! I was one hot chick well before I became aware of it.

I was spotted at the mall when I was all of fourteen. There we were, just hanging, the three of us, doughnuts in hand, checking out the boys. Suddenly this man came up to us in torn jeans and a T-shirt that had a flaming guitar on it.

"How old are you?" He asked, looking me up and down.

"What's it to you?" I shot back, checking *him* out. Not half bad, I thought. I was in the market for a boyfriend, just having got rid of the last no-hope loser I'd been dating.

He laughed and handed me a card. "Call me," he winked and walked away, whistling.

I clutched at the card gawping at his retreating back. When I finally looked at it, it had the name of an agency written in a discreet black script.

Modelling! My friends teased me mercilessly (and with a little hint of jealousy). Pa didn't want to know. Ma just spitefully spat out, "What's so special about *you*?" If it hadn't been for Nanna, I would still be in Hicksville. Nanna, who packed my little case, who paid my bus fare to the city, who kissed me goodbye, and wished me luck.

The world of modelling was hard. It was the time of the Supers. Super long legs, super toned bodies ... and then, there was little ole me - all tits and ass. Needless to say, not a lot of catwalk work came my way. Dreams of Milan and Paris stayed just that - dreams. I got good catalogue work though. There was a lot of standing around, looking cheery in dreary clothes for dull housewives. Decent money but I was bored. So bored and lonely.

Then I met Nina. She was as fair as I was dark, as experienced as I was fresh. Her blue eyes had a mischievous twinkle that only hinted at the crazy chick that lived within. We were paired in a catalogue shoot and I couldn't stay immune to her gregarious nature for too long.

"Hey hun! Whatcha doin' after the shoot tonight?"

"Cuppa Noodles?"

"B-O-R-I-N-G! Why don't you come out with me? I could show you some sights."

Boy, did she show me some sights!

So I started to party. We went out every night, Nina, and I - best friends, gal pals, homegirls, *mamacitas*! We hit all the hot spots. We were young and gorgeous, and life was one big carnival. I did all that there was to do. Drugs - check. Booze - check. Men - oooh! Double-check! It was a mad, bad and exciting world ... and I loved every minute of it!

In the midst of it all I bumped into Barry. Older, successful, married, but what did I care? It was a potent enough combination and I fell for him big time. He told me to quit partying and I did. He told me to stop modelling and I did. Had he told me to take up crocheting, I probably would have. I was getting tired of the partying anyway and was ready for a bit of cosy domesticity.

A kept woman, I revelled in all the attention Barry showered me with. Generous beyond my wildest dreams, he lavished me with jewellery from Tiffany's, scarves from Hermes and bags from Chanel. My every wish was his command, and I wished a LOT in those days. I was nineteen, and I was living a life that my friends would've given their left arms for.

Nina warned me though. "Honey, you're just his plaything. Have fun with it, but don't give up the day job."

I dismissed it as jealousy. What did she know? He was going to leave his wife and kids. Of course, he was. She couldn't give him what he wanted, whereas I could, and did, and often at that. The fact that the sex was funny and he had me do ... Oh, I won't go there! A small price to pay in the grand scheme of things.

Then I fell pregnant.

"Who's the father?" He demanded viciously, before turning me out into the street.

True love? The sonofabitch didn't even let me keep a measly scarf.

Homeless and jobless, I turned to Nina, but she turned away, cold and indifferent. Some best friend!

There were only so many couches I could sleep on before all the favours had been called in. I hadn't exactly endeared myself to people in my 'Barry days'.

From there it was an easy slide into the world of 'Glamour Modelling'. Not a lot of glamour, but a whole lotta skin. I wasn't showing my baby bump yet so I figured, might as well make the moolah uncovering the assets that I'd previously made money covering up. Also, I'd convinced myself that there was a charitable element to it all. Wasn't I bringing a bit of joy into the lives of sad and lonely men?

I would lie there in those crummy studios, with all my bits on display. Then I would zone out. Beam myself right onto a beach with a margarita in my hand. I wouldn't even feel the hands groping me, 'adjusting' me, propping me up, so that the camera could get an eyeful.

These days, I could've launched a career off the back of it. Look at good ole Hef's girls ... celebrities in their own right! But that was back then. Glamour modelling was seedy, something girls from 'nice' families didn't do, even though *nice* isn't exactly what I would've called my lot.

I lost the baby at a shoot. I still remember the look of horror on the photographer's face.

"What the fucking hell, man?! Get her off the bed! SHIT! The sheets are ruined ..."

I weighed a hundred pounds when I first started to comfort eat. Pa would chew his tobacco and watch me silently. Ma would surreptitiously replace the empty tubs of ice creams with new ones. Nanna would weep silently and pluck at my hair saying, "Oh child, oh my pore child ..."

My food orgy lasted a year and at the end of it, I was 224 pounds and officially huge. I lived in Pa's XXL T-shirts watching daytime TV till my eyes hurt. My thighs chafed when I walked, my tummy wobbled, and I could no longer see my feet in the shower. I was twenty-two going on fifty-two.

At first, my friends came to visit and gloat.

"Well, I always told ya it wasn't a good idea to run off to the city!" smirked Cindy, bouncing her two-year-old on her knee, while Debbie and Mary Lou nodded in agreement. "You coulda been married and happy ..."

I looked at her too-tight dress, the dribbly baby, and the shiner she was hiding under acres of concealer, and turned away.

They soon stopped coming over, and I didn't miss them. Not one bit.

Food was my only friend and it stuck by me, unlike the Ninas and the Cindys of the world. But Nanna worried about me constantly, urging me to eat less. "Go exercise, child! Go for a walk, I'll come with ya."

I tried a few times with Nanna hobbling painfully behind me. Then Nanna fell ill and TV took over again. I mindlessly munched through bags and bags of potato chips, listening to Nanna cough in the room next door.

I started my first diet the day after Nanna died. I ate nothing.

New York City didn't frighten me as much the second time around. The castings did. I felt a hundred years old next to the sixteen-year-olds with their fresh faces and pliable bodies. I was way past my sell-by date and they sure weren't shy about telling me that either!

Television was slightly more forgiving. A bit part here, a walk-on there. Then came the big break! An audition I aced not because of how I looked, but how I laughed. My loud mid-western guffaw caught their attention. So, with a dirty laugh and a sinful body, I landed my first major role.

Our sitcom was a slow burn at first. The lead actor Doug had great comic timing, and I was his perfect foil. With chemistry that fizzed and bubbled, it was only a matter of time before we had captured the public imagination. Then there was no looking back.

Doug: "Well, hello there! Where have you been hiding all my life?"

Me: "Somewhere you couldn't find me. Now get me my drink and make it quick!"

[cue studio laughter]

Those were great days. Halcyon days. I was young, I was hot once again, and famous to boot. A fuck was just a fuck now. I didn't care for a *relationship* anymore.

Doug, my co-star and I, became great buddies, our mutual and platonic love translating into several seasons of a hit sitcom. So much so that the tabloids had us eloping, marrying and splitting up every second day. Course, the fact that he was as queer as a three-dollar bill seemed to have escaped everyone's notice, and who was I to disabuse anyone of their notions?

The film offers started pouring in soon enough. I was wary but Doug convinced me to give it a go, and I trusted his instincts enough to agree. Sifting through the various scripts, I was left with two viable options - an action thriller with a young, upcoming actor, or a comedy with a has-been trying to make a comeback. It was a no brainer.

Contrary to subsequently embellished stories, shooting the movie was no picnic. We never really hit it off. He was too full of his impor-tance, as I was of mine. After all, I was giving *his* career just the fillip it needed! Those months were fraught with all sorts of petty indignities he would try and heap upon me. From speaking over my lines to eating garlic just before he kissed me. From ignoring all my cues, to conve-niently forgetting to attend rehearsals, he was a *fleabag* to work with. It was clear for all to see that his humongous ego couldn't cope with resurrection at the hands of a woman, a TV artiste at that! He had nothing on my Ma though. Years of living with her had given me skin as thick as hide. All of it just rolled right off my back.

The film's runaway success caught everyone by surprise. It made Mr Has-Been the biggest name in town once more, and me, his new best friend. We went on to do two more films together but didn't manage to make celluloid magic again. Pity! Never received another Christmas card from him after that.

I was thirty, huge and happening, a bona fide star! I was also battling the bulge secretly but no one except Doug and my publicist knew that.

Ma and Pa, and that wretched past seemed so far removed from my glittering life, this shiny present, as to almost never have existed. My sitcom was going great, film offers were pouring in aplenty and I was ready to make the leap from Television star to full-fledged Hollywood megastar.

When the headlines screamed - "Tonya gets her nipples out!" I was genuinely confounded. All that seedy back-alley stuff had been so long ago that I had obliterated it completely from my memory. But someone else hadn't. Now they were doing a bloody good job of cashing in on it by selling the pictures to whichever magazine bid the highest. I was, after all, a bona fide star!

It took three months for the furore to die down. I had to stay holed up in my apartment while the 'suits' did damage control. So, to fill up all that time I turned to my old friend - the refrigerator.

When I finally emerged, the shocked script-writers had to hastily incorporate a pregnancy storyline into the sitcom. Twenty pounds are difficult to disguise on camera. Add to it the ten it puts on anyway and I looked like I was ready to deliver in the next episode.

*Doug: "A one night stand and **this** happens? What if I married you?"*

*Me: "Well, if all your other swimmers are as good as this one, we'll have a soccer team in no time. Not that I'd marry **you!**"*

In a bid to make me shed the weight pronto, I was put on a diet. Atkins was all the rage in Hollywood and I was banned from eating carbohydrates. A 'minder' would come home and clean out my refrigerator of any offending items daily, but I could stuff my face with steaks, eggs, cheese and butter, all the protein that I could stomach. My breath stank, I smelled foul and Doug refused to kiss me onscreen. Regardless, the fat melted away like butter sliding off a cob of corn.

Slim again, I took up exercise quite seriously. An action movie was next and I martial-trained my way into serious abs and biceps, gracing cover after magazine cover in skimpy outfits highlighting my hard-won body. The tabloid's darling once again, my little blip was soon overtaken in public memory by the shenanigans of poor little heiresses and junkie rock stars. I couldn't help but chuckle at the fickle nature of it all.

It was at a film premiere that I met Rob. The attraction was instant. Like a movie scene where you spot your soul-mate across a crowded room while 'Some Enchanted Evening' plays in the background, our eyes met outside the Regency Theaters in Westwood Village, and everything and everyone else was instantly forgotten. We fell in love and in bed almost simultaneously. We also didn't leave the hotel room for five days and by the fifth, he'd convinced me to marry him.

I had the biggest, glitziest, craziest wedding in town. From ice sculptures in the garden to champagne fountains, from toddlers dressed as cherubs to near-naked angels serving the drinks, it was as OTT as it could get. Why not? I could afford it. Besides, it was Hollywood. So fucking Hollywood.

> Rob: *"You are my sun, my moon, my twinkling star. You are my everything. I have loved you before I even met you. I will love you today, tomorrow and all the tomorrows there will be."*
>
> Me: *"My darling! I have waited all my life to say this to someone. I love you with all of my heart. Our love is forever, eternal, etched in the stars before we were even born. We were meant to be. You are my reason, my life, my entire being."*

We'd written our wedding vows together, practising them for hours in front of the mirror, promising each other that we'd grow old together, sit on our porch and watch our grandkids play in the yard while we sipped on our iced teas. Ha! We only lasted thirty-three days. Then the bastard sued me for half of everything I had and won the bloody case too! Yeah. So fucking Hollywood.

. . .

My career nosedived shortly after. Who wanted an ageing, overweight (did I mention my weakness for donuts?) diva anymore when there were younger, prettier, more willing-to-spread-their-legs models around? They were putting me on the shelf before I was ready!

Angry, I developed a taste for French macarons, having them flown in from Paris especially for me. Tiny little mouthfuls of heaven, they were so airy and light that I figured they couldn't do too much harm. French women were so slim and they ate cheese and macarons all day long, didn't they? So why couldn't I!

The weight gain was insidious. A pound here, a pound there, and one day I woke up sixty pounds heavier. Now, how the hell did *that* happen?

Then there was Consuela, my housekeeper, who made the most *amazing* tacos. I'd rediscovered Mexican food in all its greasy glory. Refried beans! Mmmm ... just the thought of them made my mouth water. Nutty *bunuelos*, *tres leches* cakes ... naughty, naughty desserts that settled comfortably around my already ample waist.

We were a good partnership - Consuela and I. Much like Doug and I had been, until our chemistry fizzled out after that unfortunate episode in the public toilets.

HEADLINE:
Male TV star caught in a compromising position with a young man.

Really!! I thought Doug would've had classier stomping grounds. Well, never mind. No surprise then that our now-tepid sitcom stuttered to a premature halt. Doug was sent to rehab to be 'cured' of his affliction and I was sent packing with false promises of being called back if a suitable project emerged. Yeah, wasn't placing any bets on either scenario!

But Consuela and I. Now that was a partnership built to last. She cooked and I ate. It was *fabulous!* Until I discovered that while I lay corpulently supine by the pool, she also robbed. Little bits of jewellery and cash that kept going missing until I zeroed in on the culprit.

Out went Consuela. In came Jorge, whose pool cleaning capability and six-pack abs I much admired. Cooking ability? Not so much. But it was all I could afford and I wasn't going to start cleaning the pool on my own, was I?

Funds were running low and I was thrashing about looking for work. When the offer came to advertise a weight loss plan, I grabbed it with both hands. Lose weight and earn money doing it? Seemed too good to be true.

Guess what? It was.

Oh, how I suffered those eight months. The portions were tiny. I mean *tiny*. The food tasted like cardboard and I had another bloody 'minder' living with me. Watching me hawk-eyed so I wouldn't stray off the plan. Daily bloody torture.

Of course, all the while I had to appear on television and in magazines, smiling broadly, endorsing those awful, *awful* meals.

Ah! The things we do for dough.

> *"Have your cake and eat it too,*
> *Have a slice or have two!*
> *We deliver to your pad,*
> *and it doesn't cost too bad!*
> *Slimmer and slimmer you will get*
> *Weight loss woes you'll forget ..."*

Poetry it was not. But it brought home the bacon, or in this case, something that masqueraded as bacon.

I knew that I was never going to regain my teenage figure. After all, I was facing forty and really didn't mind carrying an extra ten pounds on my derriere if it made the frontier look better. After all, none other than Catherine Deneuve had famously said, "At a certain age, you have to choose between your face and your ass." Face over ass, my pick was clear enough!

Around this time, I had an offer to guest-star as the mother to one of six very famous 'friends'. I was mortified! I knew for a fact that one of them was just a few years younger than me. Mother! Me? I hemmed and hawed, finally realising that pride came before bankruptcy. However, by the time better sense kicked in, the part was long gone.

Now that food could no longer be my 'fix', I found a replacement. I'd recently acquired a laptop in the hope that it would bring me into the new century more seamlessly. Google was the first buddy I found on it.

I'd google myself - over and over again. At first, there was no dearth of information. There were photos of me at nineteen, grinning vacuously into the camera, wearing those awful frumpy clothes, with shoulder pads you could knock someone out with. My bare-assed ones surfaced too. "Tonya gets her nipples out!" apparently still got lots of hits. There were movie stills, catalogue shoots, tabloid snippets ... it was all there and it was all *so* fascinating to read. Like reading about a really famous person and then realising that it's *you*, really really *you*!

Slowly, however, it dawned on me that there was nothing new at all. No one seemed interested in me anymore. It was like circa 2005, I had *died*. Most annoying!

It was time to drum up some publicity and I did the next best thing to actually dying. I decided to adopt. It had created a lot of good press for some contemporaries I knew. Orphans, especially from very poor parts of the world, could raise my profile just enough to rekindle an interest in me. And who knows where that would lead? A new sitcom maybe, or a movie even! Yes, the world could be my oyster again if I pulled it off.

Looking through my options, I figured that the obvious countries had been done to death. Where could I go? As far-flung a country as possible? India! That's it. I could always say I was embarking on a spiritual journey - and come back with a baby and a dot on my forehead. Why, they could probably film me doing it! I could put on henna tattoos, bathe with elephants ... do all that, ya know - stuff!

My agent shot it down straight away. "Logistically not possible to adopt easily," he told me grim-faced, arguing that the adoption fever was waning anyway. "Look for another angle," he said dourly.

"Look for another job." I replied sullenly.

Ah, well! I was never the maternal sort anyway.

Retirement is a particularly difficult job in Hollywood. Fame is addictive. Once you've had it, you want more and you'll do anything to get more. I was nipped and tucked and Botoxed to within an inch of my life, but there was still no work coming my way. What was a girl to do?

So, I did what any self-respecting starlet in Hollywood would do. I crashed my car while over the limit. My mug shot was the nicest photo I'd had taken in a while. My hair was nicely coiffed, my lipstick and mascara in place. It only got a photograph on page thirty-nine. To add insult to injury, I was given Community Service by the disapproving judge. No prison sentence? No ankle bracelet? What was this world coming to?!

I had almost given up on it all when the call came. Would I participate in a Reality Dance Show? *Would I?* Hell, I would!

That was three months ago. I'm on the show now - tauter, fitter, and hours of rehearsals later, my two left feet have miraculously been traded in for some semblance of a dancer.

The rehearsals are a *bitch*, the judges are harsh, but the audiences love me. I play to the gallery and they love my bawdy routines. They love my booty jiggling, they love my raucous laugh ...

"Well really, don't you think she deserved more than 21? Yes, technically she's not perfect, but there's a certain 'je ne sais quoi' about her. I predict she's gonna stay on. This one's gonna last the distance ..."

Yep! The presenters may love me but the judges consistently score me lower than my competitors. My dancing partner tells me of conspiracies and backstage gossip. I don't care. I am in it to win it. If that means treading on a few toes, so be it.

I look around the dressing room and realise that this is where I belong. My life may have been a roller-coaster, but it's been *my* roller-coaster. The highs and lows, the failures and successes have once again brought me here - to the brink of fame, success and money. And I cannot lie. It is a place I like a lot. So much that I will do anything to stay here. Be good or bad, happy or sad, serious or ridiculous, just to keep a firm grip on this greasy pole of stardom.

Oh, and I have been good. So good! Given up all the naughties voluntarily. No chocolates, no booze, no doughnuts, no tacos ... I've turned away from them all, realising for the first time that will power is a muscle that needs as much exercise as any other. I'm looking and feeling fabulous. And it's within my grasp ... **victory!** ... I can smell success, I can feel it, I can touch it ... I can almost taste it too ...

Damn! That's not success, that's the bloody chocolate! How did it find its way into my mouth? I should spit it out. I *could* spit it out. But maybe I'll just chew ... mmmm ... and swallow... Oh, and there's more where this one came from.

Another one can't hurt, can it?

UMAMI

MARY

"So, tell me again, what does this Miss Elizabeth of yours do?" Scott looked over at me, one hand on the steering wheel and an eyebrow raised in amusement.

"She's a taxidermist," I mumbled, choking slightly on my half-eaten sandwich.

"A taxi driver? Like Uber? Is that safe to do, at her age?"

I play-punched him on his arm, giggling.

"Shut up Scott! You know what a taxidermist is. She stuffs dead animals. Preserves them for posterity. That sort of thing ..."

"So presumably, she has a lot of these dead animals about her house as well?"

"Yes. But it's not creepy. It's charming. Really, why are you being like this about her? You haven't even met her yet!"

"Like what, honey? I'm just curious about this batty old aunt of yours."

"She's not my aunt. Not a blood relative, more like a substitute grandma. Anyway, concentrate on the road. It's getting dark, and I don't want to miss the slip road to her place."

I was nervous and I think Scott sensed it. Not for the reasons that he believed, though. Yes, Miss Elizabeth was the only 'family' I had left after Mam passed and I hadn't taken a man to her place before. She was bound to be judgemental, she always was. But it could cut both ways. What would Scott think of me after meeting her? We had only been dating three short months, and I wanted him to see the best of me at all times. I wanted him to see me as cool, collected, organised, and in charge of my own life and destiny. Hadn't he said that he liked independent women?

Miss Elizabeth had seen all sides of me. She had seen me on my knees and picked me up and set me back on my feet. She had seen me in my rawest, most vulnerable state, and given me solace. I didn't want Scott to know about that. It was too early for any of that.

"So, why are we eating these sandwiches if we are going to hers for dinner, hey?"

"Scott!" I groaned, "I've told you. She's not the best cook. She's enthusiastic, but ..."

He laughed then. "I'm only teasing, pumpkin. I don't care what I eat, as long as I'm with you."

I looked outside at the darkening skyline and smiled at my reflection in the window. This was going so well. I hoped nothing would ruin it.

SCOTT

She was just so goddamn beautiful. From the first time I spotted her in the coffee shop, to when I 'accidentally' knocked her books out of her arms, I had been captivated. I played it cool. It was the only way, with girls like her. She thought she was the lucky one to have landed me. Little did she know.

I sneaked a quick peek at her. Her profile was like an ice-blonde Grace Kelly. A glacial beauty. A touch-me-not. How different she was in reality! Warm, funny, unaware of her effect on men and unconcerned about her looks. I was taking it slowly. She had been skittish as a colt in the beginning. It had been a strange push and pull game, where I had to pull without making it obvious. Till I finally reeled her in.

Yet it was I who was left reeling. Falling in love had been a strange experience. Suddenly, nothing mattered more than her. All thoughts of self-preservation evaporated. All caution was thrown to the wind. Years of self-discipline melted away. I wanted nothing more than to spend the rest of my life with her.

This Miss Elizabeth of hers, however, worried me a bit. Most women succumbed to charm and flattery, but not if they were a bit *off*. A spinster in her 70's, a taxidermist who lived in the middle of nowhere sounded a bit *off*. I'd really have to gauge how much charm to apply without coming across as too smooth.

"Tell me about Miss Elizabeth. How did you get to know her?"

She turned and smiled at me.

"She was our neighbour. She used to be a midwife. She helped my mum when she was pregnant with me and they became really good friends after."

"And what have you told her about me?"

"Just that I'm bringing a friend to dinner." She chewed on her lip a bit. "It's been a while since I saw her and I'd really rather she met you first before forming an opinion."

Her nervousness was palpable. I gave her hand a little squeeze.

"Hey, it'll be okay. She'll love me, I promise. You'll be fighting her for me soon enough." I grinned at her expression, as she punched me on the arm again. God, I loved this girl.

MARY

When Miss Elizabeth sold her semi in our London suburb and bought the barn conversion in Dorset, I'd really thought she'd gone cuckoo. For a woman of her age to choose isolation wasn't healthy. She needed people and community; a church where she could volunteer. She'd laughed at my concerns.

"My dear," she'd explained wryly, "I've had my fill of people. Especially the 'churchy' types. Hypocrites, all of them! I'd rather surround myself with nature and animals. What's unhealthy about that?"

Three years later, she was indeed thriving. Lily, her mini Schnauzer kept her company. They went for long walks together. They collected dead animals and birds. They listened to music, whilst Miss Elizabeth devoted her time to her lifelong passion for taxidermy. She was ruddy-cheeked and strong of limb. The grey pallor of hospital lighting had long since faded from her face.

What would she make of Scott? He was handsome of course, but she had never been one for outside packaging. He was charming and caring and made me laugh. I hoped she would see that, and wouldn't be too harsh. Miss Elizabeth had never had time for men. She'd had her heart broken a long time ago, Mam had told me. Since then, the foolishness of love and romance held no appeal for her.

"There, there!" I indicated. "That's the turn-off."

My heart started beating unevenly. Why was I so nervous? Even if she didn't like him, would it really matter? After all, I owed her nothing. Except for my life and my sanity.

SCOTT

We'd left the motorway and were cruising through a small village. The sunset bathed everything in a warm, orange glow. It was postcard-pretty, with little curving lanes, wisteria-covered houses, the usual pub filled with people enjoying their first drink after a hard day's work. Friendly people, simple people, people who knew nothing of the cut and thrust of living and working in the city. It was idyllic. The sort of place you wanted your children to grow up in. It was beautiful, and it turned my stomach.

"Scott?" Mary looked at me inquiringly. "What are you thinking about? You were miles away ..."

I smiled at her. It was too early to tell her. Maybe someday when I trusted her more, or maybe, when I trusted myself enough.

"Nothing much ... just how lovely it all is."

"It is, isn't it? I so envy people who live in places like these. I grew up in a semi-detached two bedder, with nothing to relieve the monotony but the planes that flew overhead."

"Your mum worked at the airport, right?"

"Yes, at security. It wasn't the most glamorous job, but it paid the bills."

"And your dad?"

She seemed to be willing to reveal a bit more about herself today, and I was eking out the details gently.

"My Da ..." She sighed. "I only saw him twice. Once when he came to collect his football stuff from the house. I must've been five. And then, the second time ... right at the very end ..."

"The end of what?"

She clammed up suddenly. I knew not to push her. It wouldn't work. Instead, I concentrated on the road. Dusk had fallen, the village was long behind us and now we were in uncharted territory.

MARY

I knew I was being difficult. Scott had tried many times before as well to ask about Da. I just couldn't talk about him. It wasn't just the abandonment. I was scarcely alone in having been brought by a single mother and an absentee father. Scores of my school friends grew up in similar environments. No, it wasn't that. How could I explain it all to Scott? How would he view me after?

We hadn't been entirely honest with each other. We were willing to share our thoughts and our bodies with one another. Yet so unwilling to share our histories. Why? What was *he* hiding?

"Scott, look out for a sign on the right. It should say 'Steeplechase Lane'. Any minute now."

I peered through the descending darkness. I had only ever driven here in the daytime. Everything seemed so much more mysterious in the dark, a landscape that was suddenly shorn of its innocence.

"I see it," he remarked and swung into the lane that would lead us to Miss Elizabeth's house.

SCOTT

The lights were blazing in all the rooms as I pulled into the drive. How odd, it occurred to me, that a woman living on her own would have all the lights on. Pensioners were normally careful with their bills. Unless she had money to burn. Mary seemed to read my mind.

"It's an old habit of hers. She keeps all the lights on."

"To chase the monsters away?" I chuckled.

"Come on Scotty, don't be mean!"

Smiling at her, I gave her hand another squeeze. For this girl, I could endure an evening with an eccentric old woman.

I took the flowers and wine out of the boot, as she reapplied her lipstick quickly. Her powder blue dress had pink geraniums on it. The lipstick matched the pink. Little details that had never registered with the women I'd dated before. She'd put her hair in a poofy ponytail that looked terribly chic. I preferred her hair down, but couldn't deny how beautiful she looked this evening. She caught me staring and blew me a kiss. Then she indicated with a tilt to her head that we'd better hurry.

I stood slightly behind her, balancing the wine and the flowers, as she rang the bell and then used the knocker to reinforce our arrival. A dog started barking behind the door.

"Down, Lily!" A husky voice commanded. Then the door swung open to reveal a woman in her early 70's, holding her dog by its collar.

"Scott!" I heard Mary scream as the ground reached up to meet me.

MARY

His skin was leached of all colour. Between Miss Elizabeth and I, we had managed to drag him into the hallway of the house. Lily kept circling him, whimpering. Miss Elizabeth was using a cold compress on his forehead and had elevated his feet on a little footstool.

"Has this happened before Mary?"

"No, not in all the time I've known him ..." My voice trembled as I looked down at him, so pale and helpless.

"Then not to worry. It could be stress-induced or low blood pressure. He should get checked out, but he looks like a healthy young man. Oh, he's coming around."

Scott groaned a bit as he moved his head to the side. I stroked his forehead, and whispered, "It's okay, I'm here. Don't worry."

His eyelids fluttered open. He looked confused, tried to sit up and fell back again.

"Don't let him get up yet Mary! I'm bringing a glass of juice for him. A sugar infusion until we get to the bottom of this."

I nodded and watched her walk briskly to the kitchen.

"Scotty, my darling, what happened to you?"

The colour was returning to his face. His eyes met mine in recognition. Embarrassment replaced the confusion.

"Did I just pass out Mary? Bloody hell! How long was I gone for?"

"There is no need for such language, young man! You were unconscious for just a couple of minutes, or else I would've been dialling 999. Here, drink this."

I noted his bemused expression as Miss Elizabeth held him up, forcing him to drink the whole glass of juice. Then we helped him to his feet and into the living room, where he sank into the armchair with obvious relief.

"Well, that's one way to make an entrance." He looked over at me, and then sheepishly towards Miss Elizabeth.

"Darling, I'm just glad you're all right!" He was looking more like himself now. I went over and gave him a quick hug. Then I turned and gave Miss Elizabeth a hug too. She hugged me back stiffly. That had always been her way.

"You had better retrieve the wine. I managed to get to the flowers before Lily got to them."

I shot out of the room to the sound of Scott laughing softly.

SCOTT

What the devil had made me faint? That seemed to be the question of the evening. I had been given a wine spritzer to nurse when I could've done with something far stronger. I could hardly protest, given I'd been scraped off the floor just a half-hour ago. I looked around while Mary and the martinet caught up. The high ceilings were a legacy of the barn, that much was evident. What surprised me was the choice of furnishings. Everything was minimalistic, almost to the point of being spartan. Clean lines, Scandinavian furniture and a predominance of white was the background to what this woman considered art: Taxidermy.

There were birds, squirrels, foxes, owls and even a cat or two, positioned all around the room, some hanging from the walls, others perched on little tables and sideboards. Each one was stuffed to look as though it were still alive, glassy eyes notwithstanding, and in a pose that signified motion. The bird about to take flight, the cat on the prowl, the squirrel nibbling on a nut. There was expertise here, and showmanship, yet I saw no charm. It made my spine tingle to be surrounded by so much death.

"Has there been a lot of stress at work for you Scott?" Mary inquired gently.

"Not particularly. Nothing I haven't dealt with before and nothing I can't handle, sweetheart."

It hadn't been the stress or low blood sugar or any of the things that the infernal woman was droning on about. Just for a moment, I felt like I had a grasp on the reason but then it slipped away again. All I could feel was a sudden, irrational dislike of this Miss Elizabeth. Of her clinical home and all the dead fauna that inhabited it. A dislike I had to mask for the sake of Mary, a dislike that shook me more than my fainting spell had.

The woman had stopped talking and was looking at me, as though waiting for a response. Mary looked concerned.

"I'm sorry I didn't catch that. Could you repeat that please?"

"I said," she replied with exaggerated politeness, "would you care for some dinner now?"

MARY

Something was wrong. Horribly wrong. I could've cut the tension with a knife. Both Scott and Miss Elizabeth were behaving normally but I could detect the undercurrents. Was he concussed? Was she cross? What was going on?

Miss Elizabeth had set the table with her best china. I was touched that she had gone out of her way to impress my plus one. Then why did I suddenly feel like she didn't want us there anymore?

"I remember this set from Wimple Close!" I exclaimed delightedly. White with red poppies. It had brought back a rush of happy child-hood memories of dinners at Miss Elizabeth's when Mam and she had chatted into the wee hours, and I had fallen asleep in front of the fireplace.

"I've had it a long time Mary. Much before Wimple Close too."

"I never did ask you, where did you live before Wimple Close? It feels like I've known you all my life."

"Well, you have. Remember I was there when you were born, I helped deliver you."

I kept up the chatter hoping Scott would join in. He stayed stubbornly silent. I could tell he was assessing her, and assessing me alongside. I looked at Miss Elizabeth anew. Her face seemed craggier than usual, the lines on her forehead deeper, but her eyes had lost none of their fire. They snapped and crackled as they always had. They could either frighten you away or frighten your demons away. In my case, it had been the latter. I was ever so grateful, and for the first time this evening felt a prick of annoyance with Scott.

"Let me help you bring the food in. Scott can keep Lily company."

He started at my tone and looked at me askance. I swept out behind Miss Elizabeth, hoping that he would regain his good manners in our absence.

SCOTT

A headache was starting up at the base of my skull. I rubbed it gently, noticing the tender spot behind my ear. Was it my earlier fall, or was it something else? The same spot hurt every time I remembered, even though I tried not to. I had pushed the memory as far back as I could, but occasionally, something would trigger it again.

I closed my eyes with a sigh. I could hear them bustling about in the kitchen, Mary's sweet murmur interspersed with the woman's hoarse voice.

A voice I had heard before! A lifetime ago. I sat up with a start, my heart pounding, my head threatening to explode. I looked at the white plates with the poppies on them. These too, I had seen. My head was swimming with the memories it could no longer contain. I felt hot and cold alternately. Mary had just entered the room with a dish in her hand. She rushed towards me, throwing the dish on the table.

"Scott, you look awful! What's the matter?"

"I ... I need to throw up ..."

I could hear them speaking outside the bathroom in low, worried tones. I had retched into the toilet, with bits of lunch and sandwich heaved out of me till nothing but my stomach acids remained unexpelled. I rinsed my mouth and washed my face, then took a good long look at myself in the mirror. I was a thirty-five-year-old man who looked like he'd seen a ghost. Which, I suppose I had.

I took several deep breaths. I could not afford to fall apart. Not here. Not now. The day of reckoning had arrived. I was damned if I was going to mess it up.

MARY

Scott had insisted we stayed. I wanted to drive him to the nearest A&E, but he wasn't having any of it. In truth, he looked better. He was laughing at something Miss Elizabeth had said, and all that previous tension had dissipated. Had I imagined it?

"Here, let me help you." He took the salad out of her hands and set it on the table. "Everything smells delicious. I am absolutely ravenous."

Miss Elizabeth was still wary. I couldn't blame her. He was, after all, an unknown quantity. What with his fainting, his strange behaviour and throwing up, anyone would think he was an odd bod. Thankfully, hardly anything rattled her composure.

I had to admit, whatever she'd cooked up did smell delicious. She was ladling some meat dish into my plate.

"What is it?"

"Pigeon." She added potatoes and salad and handed me the plate.

I eyed it warily. I'd never eaten pigeon before.

"Mary, try it. It's really quite gamey. Very nice indeed." Scott enthused tucking into his dish with relish.

"Thank you Scott," said Miss Elizabeth, "I try to eat as much local produce and meats as possible. There is a company that specialises in game, wild birds etc. I ordered this off them. I'm glad you like it."

"What do you do with the meat of all these?" He nodded at the various exhibits on her sideboard.

"Well, sometimes they are fresh enough for me to use, but mostly I do have to get rid of the meat. I may come upon these animals or birds a few days after their death, so quite often the meat's gone bad."

"What about roadkill?"

At this, Miss Elizabeth stiffened.

Scott didn't seem to notice. "I mean, that must happen around here a fair bit? Animals run over by careless drivers. What a waste of good meat. Surely someone like you would find good use for it?"

"I don't use roadkill."

Scott had already moved on to another topic. I took a bite of the pigeon but found that it tasted like sawdust.

SCOTT

Tread carefully, I had to keep reminding myself. I had no proof except for vague memories and sensory cues. I had to establish the veracity of my own recollection. Time had eroded many details, but some remained fresh to this day. I had to pepper the evening with those clues and watch her reactions. The first one had hit the bullseye.

"Umami - that is the elusive fifth taste, a sort of meaty, savoury flavour. I'd say this dish has it in spades. May I have some more?"

I forced myself to eat more. I wanted this woman confused and wrong-footed. I felt sorry that Mary would have to witness this, but I had no choice.

"So, Miss Elizabeth, may I call you Elizabeth, Liz or Lizzie? Miss Elizabeth is such a mouthful."

"Elizabeth is fine Scott. I don't force Mary to prefix my name, it's a habit for her."

"Ah yes, habits are such curious things, aren't they? So difficult to break. For instance, I really do believe we come full circle in life."

"Whatever do you mean?"

"Well, you are obviously a country girl, born and bred. Look how well you've acclimatised to living out here. I'm a country boy too, and I wonder if I'd want to retire to the village I was born in. I love the city though. I love the pace, the excitement, the honesty of it."

"Honesty? What a strange word to use for city living."

"Well, I meant it in the sense that there is no pretence. No hiding behind masks of civility. No communities gathering together to protect criminals in their midst."

"What are you on about?" Mary interjected with a laugh. "You never told me you grew up in the country. Whereabouts?"

I looked straight into Miss Elizabeth's eyes as I said softly, "A small village in Wiltshire called Chiseldene."

An involuntary gasp escaped her. Bingo!

MARY

I wasn't sure what Scott was playing at, but he almost seemed to be toying with Miss Elizabeth. I couldn't understand any of it and was starting to feel uncomfortable. Perhaps the quicker this dinner was over, the better.

He was leaning towards Miss Elizabeth now. "Know it? Chiseldene?"

"Can't say I do." She responded with difficulty, two spots of colour burning high on her cheeks.

"Oh but I think you do, Lizzie. After all, that's where you grew up too. Orchard Grove wasn't it?"

I looked from him to her and back again. What was this?

All pretence of eating had been abandoned. We sat at the table, an uneasy threesome. Scott, tense as a cat, ready to pounce. Miss Elizabeth cowering. Cowering? And I, uncomprehending, but knowing something terrible was unfolding here.

"Did you really think all your crimes would go unpunished? Did you think your past would never catch up with you Lizzie? Lizzie. That's what my mum called you. Lizzie, her mentor, her best friend."

"Scott!" I cried out, "Please ... I don't understand. What is this? Do you know Miss Elizabeth? How?"

"Haven't you been listening, my love? We are from the same part of the world. In fact, she was a very big part of my world back then."

He gave me a wry smile.

"I've eaten from these very same plates. I've been rocked to sleep by her. I've even been on walks with her, to pick up roadkill.

Remember Lizzie? Remember the meat we would salvage off them? You'd say 'waste not, want not'."

That was something Miss Elizabeth said often. Open-mouthed, I watched her shrink further into herself.

"But this is wonderful! Surely it is? This world is a small place after all." I tried injecting some humour. Anything to lighten the atmosphere.

"Oh yes, the world is very small indeed. Unfortunately for some, eh Lizzie?"

SCOTT

There was a part of me that understood Mary's confusion, a part that wanted to reassure her, to take her in my arms and say it had nothing to do with her, that everything would be okay. But the other part of me was too focussed on the woman sitting in front of me, too focussed on finally confronting my past. This part wanted to reach into Miss Elizabeth and rip her heart out, the way she'd done mine all those years ago. And no, I had no way of knowing that everything would be okay.

I could see her mind trying to piece things together. I waited.

"You are Emma's son?" She finally whispered.

"The penny drops." I leaned back in my chair. "Tell me Lizzie, when you fled from the village after all the chaos you had caused, did you ever stop to think about that nine-year-old boy you were leaving behind? That boy who had so suddenly and brutally been orphaned? Did you? Thought not."

Mary had gone white from the strain of trying to understand. She stood up suddenly.

"I am sick of this! Can someone please explain what is going on?"

"I will. I can." The woman said calmly. It was quite startling to see her regain her composure so quickly. She looked over at me, as though to check if it was okay. I nodded. This would be interesting. Her version of the events.

"I did know Scott many years ago. He is right in saying I was his mother's best friend, even though Emma was many years younger than me. There was a terrible tragedy in that village and I left for my midwifery course shortly after. I think Scott, as a young boy, having gone through all that trauma, had to blame someone. And I see now that he blamed me."

She turned towards me. Her eyes had regained their gleam. She spoke softly, sincerely. "Please, believe me Scott, I would have done anything to help. I even wanted to take you in as my ward. Social services didn't allow it. I am so so sorry. I wish I could have done something, *anything* to change what happened."

I started to clap, slowly. "Bravo! What a performance. No doubt you convinced everyone you spoke to back then as well."

"What was the tragedy?" asked Mary. She looked at me for an explanation.

"Well," I paused for a moment, shutting my eyes briefly, then with steely resolve, proceeded to tell her. "My mother stabbed my father to death. She was arrested, and shortly after, she committed suicide."

MARY

I stood dumbfounded for what seemed like an eternity. I could hear the clock ticking in the background, or was it my heart setting up its own tattoo rhythm?

Miss Elizabeth was looking down at her plate. Scott was staring at her and if looks could kill ...

"Why," I finally whispered, "why do you blame Miss Elizabeth?"

He looked at me, and for the first time ever, I saw the desolation in his eyes.

"My dad was in the RAF. He was often posted abroad and couldn't always take us with him. During one of his postings, my mum befriended a lady she met at church. Your Miss Elizabeth. I must have been around eight then. I remember them becoming fast friends, very quickly. They started spending a lot of time together. My mum confided in her, trusted her."

Miss Elizabeth looked up then. "She was a lovely girl, Emma was."

"Do not speak!" Scott said. "It's my turn to talk."

He looked back at me and his gaze softened.

"Anyway, my mum seemed happy and as a young boy I was happy that she had found a friend. Little did I know what a poisonous viper this friend would turn out to be."

"How?" I asked.

"It wasn't her first rodeo. She had done this before. We didn't know, as we had been in and out of the country while she had been up to her shenanigans. People tried warning my mum. She even received an anonymous letter in the post. She disregarded them all."

"What shenanigans? What had she done? You are not making yourself clear."

Miss Elizabeth stood up and started gathering all the dishes. "I don't have to sit here and listen to all this. Wild accusations that have no substance to them. You are in MY house, and I don't have to put up with this. Mary, take your friend and leave. We will talk another time."

Scott carried on, as though he'd heard none of this.

"She made a habit of befriending young women. Vulnerable women, lonely women, troubled women. Then she slowly manipulated them. Drip, drip, drip, she poured poison into their ears. She twisted the truth till they couldn't differentiate between fact and fiction. Then she made them do her bidding. She made *them* commit the crime, while she stood on the sidelines, enjoying her handiwork. Oh it was all petty stuff to begin with - a minor theft here, an assault there while she was preparing herself for bigger stuff all along, learning just how much and how far she could push. Nothing could ever be proved, as she never dirtied her own hands. But boy, did she enjoy the spectacle."

"No! No, that can't be true. You are making this up Scott! Why would you do such a thing? Miss Elizabeth has been nothing but kind to me and my mother. If it weren't for her, I would have been on the streets. How could you?" I started to sob. This was wrong. All wrong.

SCOTT

It was finally out in the open. The dreadful secret that I had carried like an albatross around my neck. I had been seen as the victim, the poor child of a criminally insane mother and an adulterous father. Even those who had suspected the truth could do nothing. There had been whispers of course, but Elizabeth's family and friends had formed a protective circle around her.

Then she had fled, and I had been nearly swallowed up by the system. If Dad's brother hadn't taken on the responsibility of raising me, I would have become yet another statistic.

Neil tried to give me as normal an upbringing as possible. His wife and children welcomed and absorbed me into the heart of the family. They were my salvation. The only condition he ever applied was to never speak of the past. I didn't. But I thought of it. Constantly.

As I grew, I started to make my own little enquiries. I went through my mother's personal effects and found the letter. I returned to Chiseldene and asked around. Some people were kind enough to supply me with information, some were angry at the injustice of what had blighted my life and the lives of others. Yet no one could provide me with the one thing I craved. The whereabouts of Lizzie.

Now, Fate had conspired to put me in the same room as the evil that had nearly finished me off. But as with everything, there was a price to pay. I could lose Mary, but she needed to know, regardless.

"Every word of what I say is true Mary. If you don't believe me, look at her face. The guilt is written all over it."

MARY

I looked at her face. A vein throbbed in her temple. Her eyes looked a bit manic. But she smiled at me and shrugged as if to say, "Poor boy. Pity him. Give him this moment."

I looked at him and saw pure hatred writ large. How could he loathe the one constant in my life? Was he unhinged or was she guilty?

"Mary, listen to me!" Miss Elizabeth willed me to look at her. "You've known me all your life. Do you think I am capable of any of these things? This man, this poor young man, has suffered because of the tragedy that befell him. But I am not to blame! It was his mother who decided she'd had enough of her cheating husband. What did I have to do with it? Emma was always a fragile sort. Maybe she finally snapped! How was I to know she would end up killing her husband?"

"My Mam killed my Da," I said slowly, thoughtfully. "You weren't there then either. But you were - before and after."

She started to stutter. "H ... h ... he ... attacked her. It was self-defence. He had always been a wife beater. You know that."

"No, I don't. All I know is what you told me. Mam died from her injuries."

"Yes, because he *attacked* her, don't you see?"

Some of her irritation penetrated my reverie.

"But what if she attacked him first?"

"Mary! I can't believe what I'm hearing. Are you really falling for this charlatan's story?"

SCOTT

White as a sheet, Mary faced Lizzie. It was a strange square-off. One so stolid, so earthy, so substantial. The other so slight, so evanescent, so brittle.

My mind was racing to comprehend what had just happened. Was Mary a victim of this woman's machinations too? If she was and had only just realised it, I could just about grasp the magnitude of her shock. I had lived with my tragedy all my life. I had known the perpetrator and the consequences. Mary had lived with a lie. She had relied upon and been raised by the very same wickedness that had destroyed her home.

"What were you filling in my Mam's ears, day in and day out? Were you telling her that her husband was a layabout? A good-for-nothing, hopeless wife-beater? Were you telling her what to do, and how to do it? Were you vomiting the same lies to her that you vomited to me after they were gone?"

Lizzie's face had a hunted quality to it. She took a step backwards, shaking her head.

"No, no, no. All I ever tried to do was help. Mary, you have to believe me. I raised you like the daughter I never had. I love you!"

"Love?" Mary laughed. "Not love. You fed off fear and misery and calamity. You came in shortly after I walked in on them, didn't you? I saw him on the floor, his head bashed in. I saw her sitting next to him, wounded and bloody, trying to say something to me. You grabbed me and took me out of the room. Why didn't you let me stay? Why didn't you let me hear what she was trying to say?"

"I was trying to protect you! You were sixteen. I could not allow you to stay on amid that dreadful scene."

"Yet, *you* did. You stayed till the police arrived."

"I stayed to keep your mother company."

Mary shook her head as if to clear it.

"You do have an answer for everything. What do you call a person like her Scott?"

MARY

How had I gone from believing in her to this? Had I always subconsciously doubted her? All those little details that hadn't added up - her constant regurgitation of my father's flaws, her ghoulish fascination with his death, her unwillingness to let me forget - had all signalled something else, something beyond the simple guardianship she'd provided. But how could I have put a name to something so ambiguous?

"She's a psychopath." Scott supplied. "An extremely dangerous one because you will never be able to pin anything on her. She makes sure of that."

Miss Elizabeth's face had turned puce.

"Get out!" She spat at us. "Get out, both of you!"

The veins in her neck bulged as she moved towards us, her fist raised. Lily bared her teeth at us, growling, sensing her mistress' anger.

"You come into my house, eat my food, then take the liberty of calling me names! Psychopath, am I? Very well, I AM. Yes, I enjoyed wreaking havoc in your pathetic little lives. Yes, your mother was a gutless cry baby, Scott, and yours, Mary was nothing but a whining loser. Their husbands were no better. People like that write their own fate. I did the world a service by getting rid of them."

She kept moving towards us, till her face was nearly touching mine. Her breath smelled rank, and her armpits emanated a sour odour, like yoghurt gone off. I could see bits of the pigeon meat stuck between her teeth. I recoiled and she gave a short sharp laugh.

"Try proving it, any of it! Your boyfriend's got it right, my dear. Nothing will stick."

Scott unfolded himself from the chair. He was beside me in a trice. He put his palm on her chest and pushed her. She staggered back.

"Don't you *dare* touch Mary, you evil witch!"

He took my arm.

"Let's go, honey. I can't abide being in this house another minute."

I gathered up my things quickly. We were nearly at the door when she called out.

"Wait!"

SCOTT

"Don't." I said to Mary. "She'll only play more games with your mind."

But Mary stopped and turned around, as did I.

She stood in front of us, deflated, all the fight gone out of her.

"What are you going to do?"

"We can't prove anything, you know that Lizzie. It's our word against yours. Besides, what is the point? You've done enough damage as it is. You have to live with that on your conscience, if you even have one. What we *can* do is walk away from you. Leave you to your own devices. Leave you to spend the rest of your days surrounded by all this necrosis. It has defined all of your life, hasn't it, this fascination with death and destruction?"

She shrank back, then looked towards Mary.

"You cannot leave me, Mary. You are the only family I have left."

"Watch me," replied Mary glacially.

Lizzie's face seemed to sag and then she slumped to the floor. An incoherent burble escaped her.

I rushed towards her. Lily was circling her, whining.

"I think she's had a stroke Mary. We need to ring 999."

Mary stood silently, watching me try to sit her up while searching for my phone. I felt her hand on my shoulder.

"Let's go, Scott."

"What? No! We can't leave her like this."

"Let's go."

She dragged me up. I looked at Lizzie's beseeching eyes. I looked at that white house, at the birds and animals perpetually frozen in a twilight dance between life and death. I looked at Lily, her bitch, licking her face. I looked till I could look no more.

We walked out of the house in silence.

As I drove away, I saw all the lights blazing in my rearview mirror. I glanced at Mary's silhouette, then looked back at the road in front of me.

Umami lingered on my tongue. Only now, it tasted a lot like revenge.

LOSING IT

Delhi, 1982

It was a hot and sticky day in June and Rana woke up feeling extremely uncomfortable. His pants stuck strangely to his skin, and he couldn't understand why. *Badi Amma* understood alright.

"*Arré*, look at this fellow!"

She stood over him, shaking her head as she looked at his pants and chewed her *paan*. Tiny flecks of red-stained spittle landed on him as she called out to her daughter-in-law.

His mother came in, took one look at him and his pants, turned slightly pink, and hurried him into the bathroom.

"But Mummy, I didn't wet myself. Why is *Badi Amma* angry?"

"It's okay Rana *beta*. Sometimes accidents like these happen. You are growing up *na*? Eleven in a week!"

The thought of his birthday chased all thoughts of his 'accident' away.

Two months later, while playing basketball in school, he was painfully reminded of it. It started to rain and in the downpour, Akriti's shirt turned translucent. None of the boys could take their eyes off her developing bosom.

Rana felt himself stiffen and had to run to the toilet to relieve himself. *What was happening to him?*

That evening when Papa came home from his tour, Rana approached him shyly.

"Papa, I think I'm ill."

"Come here *beta*, let me check!" Papa touched his forehead, examined his tonsils and got him to stick his tongue out. "Are you constipated?"

"It's not his stomach that's hard," cackled *Badi Amma* as she shelled the peas in front of her. "You had the same 'illness' didn't you, Ratan, when you were younger? All those socks I would find ... heh, heh ..."

Papa turned tomato red and ushered him out of the room.

"Rana, you are growing up, and umm, sometimes, men have urges ... umm, it's normal ..." he paused, "Maybe you could use tissues?"

"But Papa, my *toto* goes really hard in the mornings and sometimes in school too. What do I do with tissues?"

"Beta, you can umm, use it there like you use a tissue to blow your nose, *na?*"

Blow his *toto* like a nose? Rana was none the wiser, and Papa quickly returned to his *chai* and newspaper.

"It's simple, *yaar*," Amit said. "You think of a really hot girl. Like *really*. Then you pull and pull till it all explodes in the tissue. Job done."

Amit was six months older and a decade wiser than all the boys in the class. He watched a lot of Hollywood films on his family's newly acquired Video Player and claimed superior and *intimate* knowledge of worldly goings-on. It was to him that Rana turned when no further information was forthcoming from Papa.

"But what if it comes off?"

"What comes off - your penis? Eh, stupid boy! When are you going to grow up? Penises don't come off when you jerk off. They get bigger. That's how they grow. Don't you want a Big One?"

Rana looked at the size indicated by Amit and wondered whether he really wanted an elephant's trunk dangling between his legs. No thank you, he decided. He would put up with the pain. Never mind the tissues.

Delhi, 1983

Things hiccupped along for the next year. He was just shy of turning twelve when Rita moved in next door. Rita's mother and his own became fast friends within weeks. They were both housewives who liked cooking, knitting and gossiping. Rita was sixteen, beautiful and arrogant. Rana promptly fell in love with her.

Now, he dreamt of her day and night. He'd hug his pillow, fanta-sising it was her. He wasn't able to proceed beyond a hug because he didn't know *what* it was he really wanted.

"You need to watch a sexy film." Amit declared matter-of-factly when as per usual, Rana had unburdened himself to him. "How else will you know what goes on between a man and a woman?"

"What goes on?"

Amit and his cronies sniggered at his ignorance. "How do you think you were made?"

"Mummy and Papa went to the temple and prayed for a son. What has that got to do with my *toto*?"

He couldn't understand why they all fell about laughing. Seemingly there was a flaw in the information he'd believed to be sacrosanct all these years. He guessed he'd have to watch a sexy film. Only, he had no access to them. He didn't even know what qualified as a sexy film.

"That is a problem, *yaar*," said Amit, stroking his chin in thought. "Tell you what, there's that new fellow who has just come from *Umreeka*. Let's see if he has any ideas. These *Umreeki* boys are well ahead of us. I bet he'll know".

Indeed, Ashish, the loner, had ideas by the dozen. Grateful for being sought out when he was mostly left to his own devices on account of being different, he offered up his father's stash of porn magazines voluntarily.

"I can smuggle them in, one at a time. But you have to be careful not to get caught, or my ass is grass!" His nasal twang was both irritating and intriguing.

Rana felt very adventurous smuggling a copy home. He hastily shoved it under his mattress, waiting for an opportunity to enter that forbidden world. A world he'd only just learned existed, and that too, purely by chance.

There had been quite a hubbub in the boys' toilets in school when Ashish had revealed his little secret. Rana had been playing football and missed all the fun. The boys who had seen the magazine had all come out with a glazed look on their faces and zero concentration for the rest of the day. He couldn't wait to see what they had seen.

The cover had been promising. It was a woman in a red dress lifting the hem suggestively while biting her lip. It had made him feel funny all over.

He waited all day to steal into the bathroom, lock the door and pore over the pages of his illegal contraband. Naturally, that was the day Papa's brother and family visited.

Chitrahaar blared on the black and white television in the living room, one film song after another playing in a half hour segment. In one particular song, the hero and heroine emerged from behind a flower, looking smug and bashful respectively. He never could figure out what went on behind the flower, no matter how many times he watched that particular song.

"Rana, how are the studies going?" His uncle questioned him.

"Good *chachu*." He answered absently, biting into the cauliflower *sabzi* his mother had made. His mind was on the magazine under the mattress.

"Still want to be a doctor?" *Chachu* probed.

Rana couldn't ever remember wanting to be a doctor. It was just the stock standard answer he doled out to anyone who asked. A safe choice - the others being engineer or lawyer. He knew if he answered truthfully and said footballer, he'd be beaten to within an inch of his life.

"Mmmhmm," he murmured, concentrating furiously on chewing, hoping *chachu's* questioning would taper off.

"*Aai hai!*" emerged a shriek from his room. *Badi Amma* came out clutching his magazine. He nearly choked on his *chapati*.

"Such filth! Men with such big *dandas*, and these women ... No shame, I tell you! Doing all this baby-making thing and letting people photo them. What is the world coming to?" *Badi Amma* wailed dramatically, holding the magazine to her chest, clearly having rifled through the entire thing.

Both her sons sprung up to grab the offensive item from her. His auntie swiped it from right under their noses. She took a quick glance inside and then tucked it firmly under her arm. Turning her beady eye on him, *chachi* asked, "Where did you get this from Rana?"

"It's not mine!" The lie escaped his lips involuntarily.

"Are you sure? What was it doing in your room then?"

Mummy sprung to his defence. She had never liked her sister-in-law. "If Rana says it's not his, then it is not. My *beta* never lies."

She soon realised the chink in her defence when everyone turned to look at her husband. Papa turned white.

"That's not mine!" He shook his head vigorously. Five pairs of eyes glared at him, while one guilty heart felt really sorry, but not sorry enough to own up.

A month later, tranquillity had finally returned to the household. Mummy had actually spoken an entire sentence to Papa, *Badi Amma* had stopped talking about the horrors of the western world and Rana's bottom had stopped hurting from the thrashing it had received.

Ashish, however, had been less than understanding about the loss of the magazine.

"They *burnt* it? What the heck man! That was my dad's. How am I going to explain this?"

Rana mouthed sorry for the umpteenth time and backed away.

Ignorance was bliss, he'd decided when the ruler had connected with his backside repeatedly. He neither cared nor wanted to know any more about the mysterious contents of the erstwhile magazine.

· · ·

Delhi, 1989

"Still a vurrgin?" Amit took a swig from his beer bottle, offering him some.

Rana shook his head, refusing the beer. They were sitting inside Amit's car, waiting for football practice to begin. He felt suffocated and slightly sick. Amit's cologne always had that effect, particularly as he believed in drenching himself.

"It doesn't matter."

"Doesn't Poonam - you know?" Amit winked lasciviously at him. Rana didn't really care to talk to him about Poonam. As it was, he himself didn't quite understand his equation with her.

She blew hot and cold all the time. One minute they were going steady, the next she didn't want to know him. One minute she was plunging her tongue into his mouth, the next she was pushing him away.

"Shilpa and I have done it." Amit proclaimed. "Right here, in the car, two nights ago ... and man, it was good."

Rana looked at him enviously. Amit had certainly been born under a lucky star. Wealthy parents, good looks, an indulgent sister who lived abroad, and an endless supply of ready and willing girlfriends. What he wouldn't do to trade places with him!

"Oh, you're so naive, Rana!" Poonam put a stick of chewing gum in her mouth while watching the movie trailer. "Shilpa has done nothing of the sort. He *wanted* to and when she refused, he decided to spread these filthy lies. Amit is a sore loser, don't you know?"

He felt a little less of a loser himself when Poonam consented to hold hands for the duration of the film.

As they walked to the bus stop together, he finally broached the subject uppermost on his mind.

"Will you be my date for the Farewell party, Poonam?"

She looked at him assessingly then shrugged. "I'll think about it. I might just go with the girls. You know my parents don't approve of boyfriends at this age."

He knew and thought he understood, but in reality, all this cloak and dagger stuff was driving him nuts. He just wanted a proper girl-friend - to have, to hold and to love. Instead, he felt he was grasping at something just out of his reach. The more he wanted her, the farther she slipped away. He knew that 'good girls' didn't date, but how would he ever learn more about girls if he didn't spend any time with them?

Why did the information he received always have to be half-baked, sourced from unreliable quarters and in most cases, be comprised of other people's magnified falsehoods? Why wasn't anybody transparent or honest about their bodies, their needs or their desires?

"You look so handsome, *beta*." Mummy discreetly wiped her tears while patting his head, ruining his gelled hairdo. His grin quickly turned into a terrified grimace. *Badi Amma* was approaching him, armed with her kohl pencil, trying to place a big black dot on his cheek.

"Mummy, it's my Farewell! I can't have that stuff on my face. I'll look like an idiot!"

"You look like one anyway," sniggered *Badi Amma*. "Your hair is all sticking up like a cockerel. What have you done to it?"

"She means well *beta*. It's to ward off the evil eye. Okay, let me put it behind your ear. No one will see it there."

When he finally made his escape, he quickly wiped it off. He didn't want Poonam to laugh at him. He felt lucky tonight. She had agreed to be his date and if things proceeded smoothly, she might even agree to more.

They danced together most of the evening, but every so often she'd abandon him to go giggle in the corner with her girlfriends. He never could understand why girls nearly always moved in flocks, making it so much harder for a boy to approach them. But he took the opportunity to drink his Coca Cola with whatever alcohol that a smirking Amit had spiked it with.

Towards the end of the evening, he felt like he was dancing on air.

Tacitly, they slipped out of the hall into the side garden. She pulled his head towards her and kissed him with such ferocity, he was taken aback. His response was immediate, and she put her hand there stroking him and laughing alongside.

"You really want me, don't you?"

"Yes!" He groaned.

She unhooked her blouse and let him slip his hand inside. He felt her warm flesh, her nipple puckering under his touch, and felt his head swim.

The next minute he was puking all over her sari, his stomach heaving, his eyes watering, the remnants of his lunch ejected into a congealed mess. She screamed in horror stepping back, pushing at him with both hands, his vomit all over her. Then sobbing, she ran inside.

He leaned against the wall, his head still spinning, stomach and soul in turmoil. Maybe he should have left the black dot where it was.

Delhi, 1995

"Honestly man, I just don't get it. You were almost engaged, your parents approved of her, you had dated for nearly six months and weren't they family friends or something? What went wrong?" Amit asked.

What went wrong? What had ever gone right with Aloka? But the final straw was one that he recollected perfectly.

The problem had started in the car. They had parked in a lay by and started to kiss. Except that every time he tried to push his tongue in, she'd clamp her mouth shut.

"Aloka, this isn't real kissing. Come on, relax a bit."

"I don't want to get pregnant!"

"We're *kissing!* You can't get pregnant this way."

Mutinously, she'd stared ahead, all buttoned up and furious.

"Okay, alright, listen. Just do one thing ... Just hold me, please? That's safe. Just, please?"

Her hands had felt cold but good as she'd massaged the length of him. He'd felt himself relax and start to enjoy her ministrations.

His mind had circled back to Henna. To her hazel eyes, to the dimple in her left cheek and her uninhibited, carefree laughter. Henna, who was so wrong for him - older, divorced, the wrong religion. Why then did she send his pulse racing every time she stepped into his office?

Did he say her name out loud?

"Owwwww!"

Aloka's grip had turned vice-like, and it took all his powers of persuasion to make her release him.

Needless to say, they were both a bit bent out of shape after that, and in no mood to follow through with the engagement.

He couldn't reveal any of this to Amit. He'd once again be the laughing stock of their group. So, he said tersely, "She wasn't the one, Amit."

"At this rate Rana, you're gonna die a vurrgin."

Given his history, Rana couldn't argue with that.

Delhi, 1996

How were they the last ones in the bar together?

"This has to be the best part of the day. When all the work's been done and presented and we can finally kick back and relax."

She had one leg tucked under her, and was swirling the lime in her mojito. He nodded and smiled. Any time in her company was the best part of his day.

"So, how did you end up in advertising Rana?"

"Well, what I'd really wanted was to be a footballer ..."

They spoke well into the wee hours, time flying while they swapped tales, both trivial and significant. He drove her home, and she rolled down the window to let the wind whip her hair.

"You are very beautiful Henna," he remarked shyly.

"I know." She laughed.

His fingers were caught in the tangles of her hair as they kissed all the way up her stairs. She undressed in the light of the bedside lamp and his breath caught in his throat at how truly beautiful she was.

They fell on to the bed together, limbs entwined, his body reacting naturally, spontaneously to the stimulus of hers.

How often he'd dreamt of this moment: a beautiful woman in his arms to make love to. He had a checklist ready: lips, neck, collarbone, breast, stomach, thigh, then *there*.

He just about made it to her collarbone, when the crescendo came too soon, too unexpectedly. This wasn't how he'd envisioned it. He was meant to be the conquering hero, the one who climbed the summit and planted his flag there proudly. Instead, he'd stumbled at the foothills.

"First time?" She inquired softly.

He nodded miserably, eyes closed, face averted. "Never mind," she whispered, "It gets better. Here, let's try again."

Practice makes perfect it is said, and they practised all night long.

Delhi, 1997

"Mussalman se shaadi? Aai hai!" Badi Amma bemoaned the misfortune her good-for-nothing grandson was bringing upon their Rajput name. Marrying a Muslim girl was worse than eating beef.

Papa tried reasoning with him. "Rana, you need to meet other girls. You know you don't have to settle down with the first one you, umm ... errrr ... are *with*."

Mummy tried the silent treatment for weeks on end.

When they eventually thawed, he entreated, "Why won't you people meet her? I love her and that's the least you could do for me!"

For the first time in his life, he felt a passion he could not describe. Henna was everything to him. Nothing else mattered. He knew that he would overcome all obstacles, including his family's disapproval, to have her in his life. If there was anything he'd learned from Bollywood films, it was that the hero had to fight for his love, and fight he would!

. . .

Henna sat quietly, sipping her tea as she was examined by *Badi Amma*, who grumpily acknowledged that she was quite beautiful.

"You were married before?" asked Papa.

"Yes, I was. I was only eighteen, and he was a distant relative who lived in Kuwait. It was arranged by the family but it didn't work out."

Mummy shot her a sympathetic look and plied her with another samosa, while Papa grilled her with more questions on her background and family.

"We are Rajputs, and we don't eat meat." *Badi Amma* declared suddenly.

"That's nice." Henna said, looking confused. "Can I just ask, why is everyone looking at me in this manner and asking me all these questions?"

"Well, surely if you are going to marry Rana, we have every right to make our enquiries!"

"Marry Rana?" Henna started to laugh. "Oh my! Is that what all this is about? I thought I'd just been invited for *chai* ..."

Rana watched his dreams shatter once more, as Henna reassured her visibly perplexed audience that she had no intention of marrying *anyone*. They had just been having fun, 'going around'.

She patted him on his cheek just before leaving.

"Sweet Rana - don't confuse lust with love."

Amit had always said, "Lucky at cards, unlucky in love." Except that Rana seemed to be unlucky in everything.

He shut himself in the bathroom and sat on the commode, weeping softly, head in his hands. He'd barely had a few minutes to himself before the banging on the door commenced. It was *Badi Amma*, no doubt waiting to rub salt in his wounds.

She stood in the doorway, her mouth moving silently as she chewed her *paan*. Looking at him appraisingly, she asked, "*Theek hai?*"

Was he all right? Did he look all right?

Twenty-six years old with no wife, no fiancee and no girlfriend. He was a loser. No woman wanted to shackle herself to him. All his previous encounters flashed through his mind. Oh, how he'd tried to understand the mysterious world of women! How he'd tried to be a part of it. But none of it made sense anymore. Not him, not his body, not his life. What was the point?

Had he said it all out loud? *Badi Amma* thwacked him on his head.

"The point, you stupid boy, is to keep moving and keep trying! Love doesn't just fall into your lap at your will. Sometimes you have to search it out, other times it finds you. But what *you* do is put one foot in front of another, and keep going, not sit and cry like it is the end of the world. Someday you'll find the right girl. And if you don't, *hum mar gayen hai kya?* We will arrange a nice match for you!"

She shook her head impatiently, glared at him, then said, "If things like this crush you, how will you find the courage to navigate a marriage? You think a relationship is like a bed of roses? It is hard work, my boy, constant work, but work that feels like pleasure when it is with the right person. You have much to learn, *buddhu*, and life will teach it to you one way or another."

She turned a steel bucket upside down and sat across from him.

"You think we had it easy? I didn't even get to see your *Dadaji* till the day of the wedding. Imagine that! Imagine agreeing to spend your entire life with someone you have never even met. But that was how things were done in our day and look, we made it work. Your Papa didn't have much of a say in his marriage. Yes, he got to choose out of the five girls he was taken to see, and he picked a good one. But it wasn't easy for your parents either. You, you are lucky to have choices, to be able to go and do baby-making before marriage. And you sit here crying!"

The bucket slid a little and she nearly toppled off, before he reached out to catch her, urging her to switch places with him, not knowing whether to laugh or cry at all the unexpected wisdom being imparted to him in the bathroom, while his parents hovered outside, eavesdropping shamelessly.

Not fazed in the slightest, *Badi Amma* carried on as though she'd never been interrupted.

"So, this girl didn't work out. So what? There are plenty ... plenty of other pigeons in the sky!" She waved her hands dramatically at the peeling paint of the bathroom ceiling. "Everyone goes through their own failures and challenges, their heartbreaks, but we don't sit on the commode and cry about it!"

Then she put her old, gnarly hand on his head and muttered kindly, "Now cheer up, you *bewakoof*! Come outside and eat a *samosa*. Remember, this too shall pass."

As indeed, much later - in the fullness of time, in the rotundness of his belly, in his sweet and simple wife, three children and a contented life - it eventually did.

THE DENTIST

West Berlin

1976

Vasily had a toothache and Ilya wasn't helping at all.

"You need to see a dentist," he sniggered at him. Vasily decided to ignore this. One day, he promised himself, he would blow Ilya's brains out. But that day wasn't today.

A shadow moved against the window and Vasily straightened up. High time. They had been sitting in the car for over two hours. He looked through the binoculars but the figure had already moved out of sight. This was the worst bit of the job - all the sitting and waiting around, particularly with retards like Ilya.

"Vodka?" Ilya offered his hip flask.

Vasily shook his head sharply. He never drank on the job. It just made one sloppy. Ilya was proving to be a liability, he'd have to get rid of him soon.

He knew why Ilya had been ordered to accompany him. The bosses thought Vasily was becoming too big for his boots. That his 100% success rate meant he thought he was indispensable. Ilya was the watchdog. Keeping tabs on what Vasily did and how he did it. Not for long though.

The figure reappeared at the window. This time Vasily got a good look at him. Bingo! He motioned to Ilya and they slipped out of the car noiselessly.

They crossed the tree-lined street, one behind the other. To passers-by, they seemed like any other suburban commuters returning home: shoulders hunched, trench coats and hats protecting them from the mild drizzle. No one could make out the bulge of the holsters under their coats. Just as well. No witnesses.

Ilya knocked on the door. A gruff voice answered, "Yes?"

"Delivery."

"I haven't ordered anything."

Vasily had already broken in soundlessly from the rear door.

Anton turned around, gun in hand. There was a weary look in his eyes. As though he'd been expecting this for a while. As though all the running and hiding had been leading up to this very moment.

"The Dentist! Ah, I should have known they would send you."

He lowered his gun. Vasily's reputation preceded him. Besides, Anton looked tired and ready to succumb to his fate. "Make it quick, will you?"

Vasily did.

When Ilya walked in on them five minutes later, Vasily was unscrewing the silencer off of his gun.

"So it's done."

Vasily ignored him and pulled out his extraction forceps.

"It's a bit psychopathic, isn't it? This extracting of a tooth from a dead man. What purpose does it serve? He's dead. Aside from it being your *signature,* what does it matter?"

Oh, it mattered all right. Vasily hadn't risen through the ranks of the KGB on the merit of his good deeds alone. He knew the psychological impact that a well thought out name and a signature move had. It wasn't for nothing that he was regarded as the best assassin in the world to those in the know.

———

Moscow

1976

Anatoli leaned back in his chair, the cigarette dangling loosely between his lips. The file had 'ELIMINATED' stamped in red on the front page.

"Such a shame. Anton was a good man. But when spies go rogue, they have to be ..." He drew his finger across his throat. "So, Vasily, another job well done. You got his tooth, I'm guessing?"

He didn't wait for Vasily to confirm this.

"Third molar from the left, hey? What if they don't have one? What if they have rotten teeth? Those Englishmen normally do. No, no. Don't answer that. I don't really care." He placed a file on the desk in front of him. "I have another job for you." He passed the file over to him. "Top Secret, sensitive material as always." He looked thoughtful. "No killing involved this time, unless absolutely necessary."

Vasily skimmed over the information and looked up at his superior in surprise. This was not within his usual remit.

Anatoli nodded. "Yes, I know it's strange. But you were specifically asked for."

When Vasily spoke, which was very rarely, people had to lean in to listen. His voice was no more than a whisper.

"I kill people. I don't kidnap little girls."

"She's not a little girl Vasily. She's eighteen and our top gymnast. She is also planning to defect to the West sometime during the games."

Vasily looked at the photograph in the file. She looked twelve. He shook his head.

"Not for me. Give this one to someone else."

Anatoli stubbed his cigarette out leisurely.

"You don't get a choice, Vasily. The job needs to be done, and it needs to be done by you. Ilya will help."

―――――

"What I can't understand is why we are bloody kidnapping one of our own athletes? And asking for a ransom? Whose dumb idea was this?"

Vasily wished Ilya would shut up. He didn't like the plan himself, but if the powers that be had decided that this was the way to stop the defection and sully the West, then so be it.

They were booked on the next morning's Aeroflot flight to Montreal via Paris, and Vasily wanted a good night's rest before they embarked on this harebrained scheme.

Summer Olympics
1976

It was easy enough to identify the Soviet team in their blue jackets. They were all huddled together at the airport, talking excitedly amongst themselves.

Not so easy to locate a slight figure with blonde hair and blue eyes, however. Ilya spotted her first, and nudged Vasily in the ribs. Vasily moved away casually and looked in her general direction.

She was a tiny human being who could perform magical things on the uneven bars. He had been reading up on her. She was the Soviet's brightest hope at the Olympics. Just then, she looked up and caught his eye. There was a quizzical look in hers, and he looked away uninterestedly.

They were five rows behind the team on the plane. Ilya was snoring loudly next to him. Vasily looked at him disgustedly and went back to reading Pravda.

At Montreal, when her luggage went missing, she was accompanied by her coach to the Lost Luggage counter, while the rest of the team made their way out. Vasily and Ilya stood at the counter pretending their bags had not arrived either. Ilya filled out his form alongside her coach Yuri. She stood to a side, nervously rocking on her feet. The Aeroflot employee had been paid well and disappeared long enough for an uneasy silence to descend on the group. Ilya with his customary garrulousness decided to cuss out his national airline.

"Cannot believe how incompetent they are. Losing our bags is one thing. But to lose a team member's bag!"

The coach clucked in sympathetic annoyance. Soon Ilya and he were engaged in an in-depth conversation.

"Is he your son?" she asked suddenly.

"Ilya?" Vasily was startled. Ilya was young, but he wasn't young enough to be his son. "No, just a business associate."

Vasily examined Ilya with fresh eyes. He supposed, to an eighteen-year-old girl who didn't see any of his flaws, he might appear quite handsome.

As for himself, he knew he was so ordinary-looking that it made him instantly forgettable. A huge asset in his line of work.

"Which sport do you do?" he asked, feigning ignorance.

"Gymnastics." The pride in her voice was evident.

"Looking forward to the competition then?"

"Yes, of course! It's what I've spent my entire life preparing for."

The cynic within him applauded her performance. She seemed every inch a naive, eager sports girl determined to find her place in the spotlight. Not a cold, calculating turncoat, ready to abandon her country for a cushier existence in the West.

The bags finally made an appearance. By which time the Soviet team had already departed for their accommodation. It wasn't hard for Ilya to persuade Yuri to share a taxi with them.

———

She was spitting nails the next morning. He'd tied her hands and feet together but left her lying in bed so that she was, at the very least, partially comfortable.

"You bastards! Why the hell have you kidnapped me?! Where is Yuri?"

Poor Yuri would soon be found wandering the streets of Montreal, with a killer hangover and no recollection of where he'd misplaced his star gymnast.

"He's safe," Ilya spoke from the couch, munching on his potato chips.

"Why? Why ..." she spluttered incoherently.

Vasily opened the file in front of him.

"Your father is Boris Petrov?"

"Why am I here? You know I'm representing my country in the games. How can you do this? You will pay for this!"

Vasily looked at her patiently until she calmed down.

"Your father is Boris Petrov?"

"Yes," she muttered, sullenly.

"Related to David Petrov, or David Peters as he is known these days?"

She looked confused.

"Are you telling me that you don't know that your father's cousin is a Canadian citizen? Or that he's a multi-millionaire?"

She shook her head. "I have no idea what you are talking about! Please release me so that I can participate in the games. My team, my family and my friends must be so worried."

"Nice try sweetheart, but you're going to stay with us just a bit longer," chuckled Ilya.

———

There was an international outcry. For a sportswoman being kidnapped for no good reason on the eve of the Olympics made headlines everywhere.

They stayed holed up in the motel, where no questions were asked as long as cash was provided upfront.

The girl grew more and more uncommunicative. She ate at regular intervals as if only to keep her strength up. The rest of the time, she retreated within herself. Vasily admired this trait. He knew how much self-discipline it took to keep only one's own company.

Ilya, on the other hand, had no concept of self-discipline. He ate, he drank, he snored and he farted with impunity. The rest of the time he regaled them with stories from his childhood. When he ran out of those, he started to sing tunelessly.

Many a time Vasily wished it was Ilya tied up on the bed, and the girl his companion.

———

The ransom demanded was a mere two million Canadian dollars. Not too much for a multi-millionaire uncle to dole out for the safe return of his celebrity niece.

They turned the television on to listen to the news.

Tearful appeals from her parents, from her teammates, from her coaches. Nothing from David Peters.

"Is this plan actually going to work?" asked Ilya on the fourth day.

Vasily shrugged. Plans were outlines, the details were filled in by the executors. Through years of experience, Vasily knew that one had to learn to pivot if needed, amend if required, and change direction if called upon. A plan's success depended upon quick thinking just as much as quick action.

"What plan?" her ears perked up.

Vasily changed the channel to the games. He saw her sit up straighter. A part of him felt bad that she couldn't fulfil her dream, but at least she'd live. None of his previous hostages had.

On the seventh day, they had a breakthrough. David Peters agreed to pay the ransom.

———

"It's a simple matter. We collect the ransom and hand the girl over to the authorities. At that point, her profile is so high that she cannot simply melt away and defect as she was planning to do. She will be surrounded by the highest level of security. Russia will get her athlete and her ransom back."

Even as he mouthed these words, Vasily felt discomfited. Could it really be as easy as they had made it sound? There were risks. But then, there were always risks. He had been in stickier situations before and always managed to walk away unscathed. What he relied on every single time was not just preparation and nerve, but his gut.

And right now, his gut was telling him something wasn't right.

From the doe-eyed girl on the bed to his bumbling companion, to this entire kidnapping/ransom scenario he was trapped in, something felt amiss.

Maybe it *was* time to retire. This niggling feeling that had been growing more intense with every job, every passing year. Time to spend those millions squirrelled away in that numbered account in Geneva, surreptitiously acquired over the years by the 'unofficial' side jobs his superiors weren't privy to. Maybe it was time for him to melt away just like the girl had planned to.

———

The Notre-Dame church was crowded with tourists. Vasily moved along with a tour group, half-listening to the guide describing the stained glass history of the city. Pew 11 wasn't hard to find. He sat in Pew 14, discreetly observing all who were looking for him. The money had been placed in a hassock of his choosing, and now they were waiting to arrest whoever picked it up. As if.

He closed his eyes and let his head drop, seeming, for all intents and purposes, a man engaged in prayer. He had decided definitively that this would be his last job. He'd had enough. He would mail his collection of molars - 38 in all - to Anatoli anonymously. A novel resignation if he thought so himself.

The minor explosion outside the church created exactly the sort of panic he had envisaged. He walked out with the hassock in his rucksack, completely unnoticed.

The motel room smelled stale. Food, cigarettes and body odour mingled together in a fetid union.

"Did you get it?" Ilya asked eagerly.

Vasily nodded. "Check it."

He looked at the girl on the bed. "We turn her over to the authorities tomorrow."

"I'll tell them it was fellow Russians. I'll tell them everything," she declared.

"My dear," he whispered, "By the time they recover you safe and well, no one will care. By the time they care, you will be back in the Motherland."

She hissed at him then. "You've taken everything away from me!"

"Cheer up, there's always 1980 to aim for. And no sly defection ideas the next time around, you hear?"

"I'm afraid that's not really the plan Vasily," Ilya spoke softly behind him. He had the gun pointed at Vasily's head. "Did you really think we would take back a traitor, no matter how talented?" He glanced at the girl on the bed.

Vasily looked at her too. She was trembling in fear for the first time in the ordeal, her eyes pleading, turning from him to Ilya and back. He felt sorry for her, knowing that her fate was sealed.

"So, Anatoli has asked you to get rid of me too?" Vasily whispered, his voice barely audible.

They must have been on to him for a while. Hence, Ilya.

"Oh, I know what you think of me old man. But I am no fool. Don't even bother reaching for your gun. It's been emptied of ammunition a while ago."

"Emptied chambers can be refilled too, Ilya."

Montreal
1976

The crowds were cheering on television as Nadia Comaneci got the first ten ever achieved on the uneven bars.

On the floor of the motel room, there was a different kind of ten. The man's figure lay stretched out straight and the girl was curled up like a ball next to him. Their bodies were stiffening up with rigor mortis.

The television flickered in the background, noise fading in and out. They wouldn't be discovered for another week, at which point their bodies would be sent for autopsies. The man would have his third molar on the left missing, a fact that would perplex a few in Montreal, yet not be deemed salient enough to investigate. The killer had banked on this. He was aware that his trademark flourish was a private quirk that would eventually melt into anonymity alongside him, just as he had always planned.

Moscow

1976

Anatoli had not stopped looking over his shoulder since the botched operation in Montreal, when a package appeared on his desk one morning. Thirty-nine molars along with one simple message from The Dentist: "I like even numbers."

SOMEONE LIKE YOU

I am in New Orleans again. The last time was when I came here with Maddie five years ago. It was a whirlwind trip that we kicked off with a day that began with creamy café au lait and sweet, sugar-dusted beignets at Café du Monde, and ended with expensive, potent cocktails at the famous Carousel Bar in Hotel Monteleone.

It was so much fun, our joint twenty-first birthday getaway! After months of planning, and many years of anticipation, it did not disappoint.

We'd walked everywhere, inviting admiring glances our way. Eating shrimp po'boys, laughing as the sauce squirted on to our chins; looking at street art, pretending to be connoisseurs, fooling no one except ourselves. Ducking into the French Quarter for a cheeky afternoon Cuba Libre, we'd wandered through the back alleys exclaiming over the voodoo shops, the Venetian masks and the bizarre remedies recommended for everything from a headache to a fading libido. We had posted our photos on Facebook and Instagram, using filters to look even prettier than we already were. And we'd gotten loads of likes and comments. Maddie more than me, but I'd expected that anyway.

We'd always been perfect together: 'the two bombshells'. She was drop-dead gorgeous - tall and slender with waist-length, poker-straight blonde hair, a peaches and cream complexion and cornflower blue eyes. I, on the other hand, was shorter and curvier with dark, thick wavy hair, large hazel eyes that flashed green when annoyed, and full lips that declared my Colombian heritage to any casual observer. Between the two of us, we'd never been short of male attention. We'd known this since high school when our friendship first blossomed - known that separately we were attractive enough, but together we were irresistible!

Even that last night here in NOLA, we'd ended up with more admirers than we could cope with. We'd enjoyed all the free drinks they'd plied us with, flirted shamelessly with all of them, then slipped away quietly, giggling into the night. A modus operandi we'd used successfully many times before. Neither of us was ready for a relationship back then, we'd only sought out and found fun through quick and casual encounters.

This trip is going to be quieter, that's for sure. No one knows I'm here. They assume I'm in Washington D.C. on a work trip, and they know not to contact me. I've always been a stickler for going off-grid when on a new project. Not even Ma and Pa will call, which is really for the best, or I might change my mind altogether. Anyway, they have enough on their plates for a while trying to get my brother Oscar, the druggie, clean again.

I've checked into a nice hotel. Fortunately, this time I can afford a more expensive hotel, unlike our Airbnb with its lumpy mattress and leaky faucet. But that hadn't mattered back then. When you're young, comfort doesn't feature that highly on your list of priorities, although at twenty-six, I'd hardly qualify as old. But so much has changed in the last eighteen months that I *feel* old. Old and weary. As though life has beaten me around the head, and every time I've tried to get back up, it's walloped me again.

Mama Juju had predicted this, hadn't she? In that fifteen-minute tarot card reading conducted while we were under the influence, with me trying hard not to giggle and Maddie not trying at all. Strangely, I have almost total recall of that reading, as though every card, every word has been etched into my mind with indelible ink.

"Do you want her here?" She'd stuck her chin out in Maddie's direction.

"Yes, of course!" We were only doing this for a bit of fun and even though Maddie had been reluctant at first, I'd dragged her into the cave-like shop.

Mama Juju had subscribed to every cliché that had ever existed about voodoo practitioners. Her cave had been little more than a shop transformed to exhibit her many talents. Feathers and talons hung off the ceiling, keeping the many fake skulls company. A strong smell of incense permeated the air. The lights were kept deliberately low, so that none of the bric-a-brac was visible clearly, giving it all a rather spooky aspect. Garlands, talismans, voodoo dolls, potions, masks and crystal balls jostled for space. In the midst of it all, she'd sat a small table, covered by a black cloth. Shuffling her tarot cards, she'd observed us walking in, her eyes skimming over us, used to curious tourists wandering in, all sceptical and disbelieving. She'd stood up to welcome us and I couldn't help my sharp intake of breath.

Taller than I'd expected, her ebony skin gleaming in the dim light, she was clad in a floaty kaftan with a colourful scarf on her head. But it was her eyes that caught and held my attention. Large and mesmeric, as though unravelling every thought, every feeling;   decoding and dismissing the extraneous while latching onto the essence of what made you. Perhaps Maddie had felt something too, because she'd clutched my hand, an unspoken fear hanging in the air between us.

Then Mama Juju had smiled and her crooked teeth had immediately dissipated that fear, letting our previous inebriation take over once again. Giggling and elbowing each other, we'd stumbled in to have our fortunes told.

Maddie had leaned back in the chair next to me, her back curving into an insouciant C, while I'd leaned forward, curious to see what Mama Juju would predict for me. She'd asked me to pick six cards out of a deck. Then she'd placed them on the table in front of her, turning them over one by one. When she'd laid the cards face up, studied them for a while then glanced at me peculiarly, I'd felt a shiver, as though someone had trickled cold water down my back.

The cards had made no sense to me. They were all upside down anyway, with all sorts of pictures on them. She'd observed them for a beat again before looking up at me.

"This card here is how you feel about yourself," I could see a man sitting on a throne. I'd giggled a little, throwing Maddie a sideways glance but she'd had her eyes closed. Mama Juju looked at me intently. "Do you want me to carry on?"

"Yes, sorry. Go on."

"You feel that success and achievement are on their way to you. A significant man, perhaps your father, partner or boss will provide his support. He will be a very important factor. But you also have the confidence and the ability to exert an influence on others. Do not forget that."

It was true that underneath my frivolous exterior I was single-minded in my determination to succeed. The granddaughter of immigrants, I desperately wanted to prove myself equal, if not better, than my peers.

She had my attention now.

"This second card is The Death card. It signifies what you want most right now. The cards suggest that what you most want at this time is absolute change, to end what no longer works for you and start afresh. You may desire to transform your career, your love life or your entire lifestyle, but change is the way forward."

Yes, yes, I nodded in agreement, not caring anymore that this could all be some stupid con to lure tourists to part with their money.

"This here is The Fool. It represents your fears. You are afraid of making the wrong decisions. There is a warning here that foolhardy, impetuous actions could lead to major problems."

I had never been foolhardy in my life. Despite all appearances to the contrary, I evaluated every action for its risk factor, able to steer myself and Maddie away from trouble without anyone quite figuring out how I had done it. It was a caution bred into me since childhood, knowing viscerally that there was no safety net to catch me if I fell. It was also a caution I exercised having seen Oscar going down a path that had led to nothing but misery for all. Yet, my overarching fear was of making some sort of catastrophic mistake that could derail my entire life plan.

"This card here is The Chariot. It shows that you have a lot of drive. You aren't a quitter and your conflicts however difficult they may be, will almost always end in victory, so don't give up!"

She smiled at me benignly, her crooked teeth hidden behind her full lips painted a deep crimson. Then she looked at Maddie who had fallen asleep in the chair next to me, her mouth slightly open, slight snores escaping her. Mama Juju frowned, looked back at her cards and then pointed a long crimson fingernail at the next card.

"This is The Hanged Man. This shows what is going against you. You are allowing yourself to be victimised, emotionally blackmailed or used by others. Or, maybe you are the one manipulating?" She raised a questioning eyebrow at me, then shook her head as if dismissing that notion. "Someone or something has to go. Don't try to hang on for the wrong reasons. You have to find the ability to let go and give this up. Don't worry, it will turn out for the better for you." She threw another quick glance at Maddie who was stirring in her chair. "If you don't, perhaps things will not turn out as well as you want them to."

Maddie sat up. "Did I fall asleep? Are you done? I'm tired. Can we leave now?"

"Just one more card and we'll leave. What does this one mean ... this one with a circle and all these symbols on it?"

Nothing Mama Juju had said had seemed jarring or incredible, it had seemed as though she was spelling out what I had always known, subconsciously, subliminally. I had a desperate desire to find out more, to get her to shuffle the deck again, but there was no way that Maddie would sit through another reading. So, this final card was my last chance to discover another kernel of truth and I was impatient to know more.

"This here is the Wheel of Fortune. The card that determines the likely outcome. Expect your life to change quickly. Positive change and good fortune is evident here, but only if you discard that which is dragging you down. If you have important choices to make, trust your intuition. If you need outside help, seek it. Your destiny will lead you the right way."

Maddie yawned loudly, as if reiterating her fatigue. I quickly took out a twenty dollar bill and handed it to Mama Juju, mouthing a thank you.

As we got up to leave, she called out to me.

"If ever you need another reading, or anything else, anything at all, come back to me. I will help you."

Her words ringing in my ears, I'd left with Maddie, soon consigning the entire episode to the back of my mind.

Five years have gone by and yes, I've seen the career success I sought covertly at first and then, boldly, proudly. As a Latina woman I've climbed pretty high up the corporate ladder, and now, I'm ready to make the switch. Politics has been beckoning for a while and my gut has been responding in the affirmative. My family background and my brother's addiction aren't factors that will hold me back. If anything, they will make me relatable, someone who understands the challenges of our community and can represent them honestly and with integrity.

So, why am I here, wandering the streets of New Orleans, looking for a woman whose predictions had hinted at the very dilemma I face today? A woman whose forewarning I had ignored. Is this really the most politic or wise thing I can do? Yet, I know that I need answers, and if possible, a solution.

It's nearly dusk and I have wandered the length and breadth of the French Quarter and the Treme. But I cannot for the life of me remember what Mama Juju's shop was called, or where exactly it was located. I've gone into a few thinking "This is it!", only to be disappointed. Instinctively I know that they cannot provide me with what I'm looking for, even though they try, with their offers of potions and spells, gris-gris and charms. I wander out dispiritedly, still searching.

The golden glow of the setting sun seems to have lit a fire on the Mississippi River as it gleams like molten lava, shimmering as the day dies. I sit on a bench for a while, contemplating its beauty, allowing myself to mull over the many choices I have in front of me. I could leave now and just forget about it all. Or, I could keep trying to find Mama Juju and get that which I need to proceed further. Which will it be?

The answer seems to whisper itself in the slight breeze that caresses my cheek. I get up in a trance, my feet moving of their own accord, leading me to the same lanes I have wandered all day long, but this time knowing intuitively where to go. That little by-lane, the inconspicuous store-front, the name of the shop partially obscured by a tree branch ... it is exactly as my mind suddenly remembers it. I step inside and the smell of the incense is powerful, my eyes once again adjusting to the gloomy interior that has barely changed in the five years that have gone by.

And there she sits. Mama Juju. Not a day older but seeming older than the ages. Her eyes watch me with no flicker of recognition but she draws me in with her gaze, a magnetic pull that has yanked me to this very spot, as she had known it would.

"You are back." She declares this fact baldly, her face sombre in its aspect.

"Yes."

"I knew you would be."

"Then you know why I am here as well."

"Yes, I do."

"Can you help me?"

She indicates that I should sit, perhaps noticing my knees knocking into each other.

I take the chair, the same one I'd sat on the last time I was here.

"It is not easy, what you want of me. It is also very expensive."

"I have enough."

"And have you thought of the consequences? Because there will be, how do I say this ... side effects?"

"I don't care. I need it done. Everything depends upon it."

"Then I will need something of his and something of hers. Have you brought anything with you?"

"Yes, I have his nail clippings and I have a few strands of her hair."

"Any photos?"

"Yes, here is one of the both of them, together."

"That is good, that will do. Come back tomorrow and I'll have it all ready for you."

I get up to leave.

"Mama Juju, how did you know that I'd be back and what I would need?"

She looks up at me and smiles, her face creasing into well-etched lines, her crooked teeth more sinister than friendly this time.

"I could ask you the same thing. How did you know what to bring or where to find me? Nothing is a coincidence. You came to me the last time because you needed me then. This time you need me even more. I could see it in the cards I'd pulled for you, I could sense it in the fire in your belly and the hunger in your soul. You will not let anything stand in your way and I am the only person who can help you get what you want."

I had done my research before coming. In Incognito mode on my laptop, I'd looked into voodoo and the black arts, searching out means and methods that could lead to the outcome I desired. Everything had unfailingly pointed me back to Mama Juju. Had there always been a darkness within my soul; a darkness that would go to any lengths to get what it wanted? A darkness that was willing to see anyone and anything destroyed, if it stood in my way?

The next morning I call home.

"Mama, it's me. How is Oscar?"

"Ah, Vallé, *chiquita*, he is not better ... Your Papi has taken him to the facility again ..."

She rattles on, talking about Papi and Oscar, not once asking how I am. I love Mama, but know that I have never been her favourite. Oscar, her wild, unpredictable boy has always held her heart and her attention. By my very self-sufficiency I have become separate from them, this family that has bound itself like a unit over their troubles. They have never understood my ambition, my need to be recognised in my own right, or my ability to rise above by the dint of hard work and my single-minded focus. Ashamed of their background and heritage, they have hidden in plain sight, doing forgettable jobs and mingling only with their own kind. Happy to survive, grateful for the meagre opportunities, unwilling to stick their heads above the parapet for fear of calling unwanted attention to themselves. I am not of that ilk and it perplexes them no end.

She has paused, as though waiting for an answer.

"What Mama? I missed the last bit."

"Maddie was asking when you'd be back. She needs help with the wedding dress."

I feel like someone has twisted the knife in my heart once again.

"Tell her I'll be back by the end of the week."

"Why don't you call her, Valentina?" I can tell my mother is slightly annoyed now. She is getting tired of being the conduit between Maddie and me. I have used her mercilessly in the last eighteen months, citing work and travel as my excuses, avoiding facing my best friend for fear that I will not be able to hide my hurt or my anger. Mama doesn't know any of this, so she thinks I am being a bad friend, an unsupportive one who is shirking her responsibilities, too preoccupied with her own life.

"I'll call her Mama, but I'm really busy right now. I promise! Okay, I have to go now. *Te amo*. Bye!"

I hang up quickly, then stretch in bed, yawning. I feel no guilt at this stage, I am beyond all that now. Once my mind is made up, there is no looking back.

I shower and change then head downstairs for breakfast. The day has dawned bright and the morning sunshine is creeping into the buffet hall, illuminating the croissants, fruit, pastries, cheeses and cold cuts on the one side, while the chef takes orders for eggs on the other. I settle myself at a corner table indicating to the Mexican waitress that I'd like a coffee. She comes and fills my mug immediately, smiling as she does, perhaps recognising the Latina in me. I smile back absently, scrolling through the news items on my phone.

I linger over my omelette, knowing that this may well be the only meal I eat today. Will I have an appetite for food after I visit Mama Juju?

I'm still absorbed in the article when I hear someone clear his throat next to me. I look up, irritated by the intrusion. He is tall, greying at the temples, but handsome in an old movie-star sort of way, with high cheekbones and a slightly hooked nose. Dressed in chinos and a linen shirt, he wouldn't look out of place on an expensive yacht.

"Mind if I join you?"

"Ummm ..." I'm wondering how to voice my objection, but he's already pulled out the chair opposite me.

"I'm not usually this forward, but I couldn't help notice you when you checked in yesterday."

I look at him inquiringly, not giving an inch.

He shrugs, smiling slightly.

"You reminded me of someone I once used to know."

"Oh?"

"Anyway, I wondered if you'd like to have a drink with me tonight? Just a drink, nothing else ..." He trails off, looking at me expectantly.

"I ... I'm..."

"Look, I'll leave it up to you. Meet me at the L Bar at six. If you're there, great! If not, I won't hold it against you ..."

He gets up to leave, giving me a wry smile before departing. There is something very attractive about him and if my heart wasn't already entangled elsewhere, perhaps I would take him up on his offer. As it is, I know that I won't.

Will had the build of a football player, all muscle no fat. But he also had the soft brown eyes of a spaniel eager to please, the gentlest of smiles, the softest of touches, and it hadn't taken me long to fall in love. His father, my organisation's owner and boss, hadn't been best pleased with us dating, but had recognised that I was perhaps the very thing his son needed. A woman with spine and ambition. He was too soft, brought up by a mother who had coddled him from birth and then tragically died when he needed her the most, in his raw teenage years. Neglected by his career-driven father, he'd sunken into depression till he'd found that throwing himself into football was the perfect escape. The daily pummelling his body had received had healed his broken spirit in unexpected ways. But it was his fruitless search for love, for the same unconditional nurturing, that had seen him lurch from relationship to relationship until he'd chanced upon me.

I wanted to give him everything he hadn't had: the love, the care, the patience, the softness that he'd yearned for in the last nine years. But I'd also had one eye on the prize. Marrying Will would've meant marrying money. Old money. The kind that would give me just the boost I required to enter politics.

William Paley Hunter Senior was no fool, he'd sniffed out my ambition and my game right from the start. But he also perhaps understood that none of the wealthy heiresses or gold diggers *saw* William Junior. Really, really saw him for what he was. Soft, flawed and beautiful, requiring care like an orchid with particular needs. If mishandled he would most certainly wither and die. But if handled gently, carefully, with the right amount of sunlight, water and pruning, he could be resplendent.

Who says you can't mix business with pleasure? I'd loved Will with all my heart, but my brain had never disengaged from the journey I had chosen to undertake. A journey that was destined to bring us both glory but also the ability to accomplish a lot, do good and give back. All worthy goals, I'd been convinced back then, and still am.

He was just shy of proposing when Maddie had walked back into my life. Wandering Maddie, backpacking her way through Australia and Asia, had shown up on my doorstep in Boston.

Grimy, with her matted hair, and smelling like cabbage, Will had looked at her and puckered his nose in disgust. Then she'd showered and changed into a thin cotton dress, her long, blonde hair hanging down her back still damp, her face flawless and beautiful with not a scrap of makeup, her body graceful and sinuous, her smile just as dazzling as I remembered it, and I'd watched my boyfriend of a year fall helplessly in love. I'd watched my dreams splinter into a million shards as my oldest, best friend in the entire world had pulled the rug out from under my feet.

What can you say to a couple who only have eyes for each other? What can you say to lovers who break other peoples' hearts with impunity, locked in their selfish bubbles, living and breathing in tandem, as though two halves of a whole?

I'd backed away in anger and confusion. I'd buried myself in work, feeling hurt and betrayed. It was William Senior who'd understood and sympathised, and moved me up the ladder quickly. He'd opened new doors and offered me opportunities that I'd grabbed and wrung out for every drop of potential. I'd soared, seemingly unaffected by my boyfriend's defection, but inside I'd cried bitter tears of rage and resentment. Not that anyone could have known from my perfectly calm, perfectly composed exterior.

I'd even sent them a bouquet of flowers upon their engagement, which had prompted Maddie to ask me to be her bridesmaid. I'd accepted graciously over the phone, feeling the sting of her selfishness, the complete wilful ignorance of her culpability. I'd vowed then to destroy them as they'd nearly destroyed me.

It is late morning as I wander back to Mama Juju's shop. I've memorised the way now, knowing that I cannot afford to get lost again.

She's waiting for me, her hands calmly shuffling the cards in front of her. For the first time I notice that there is no one else in her shop. On the three occasions that I have been here, no one else has wandered in or wandered out. Once again, a chill runs down my spine and I wonder whether I can still back out, back away. But no. My feet have a mind of their own and they place me in the same spot that I'd stood in last evening.

"Would you like another reading?"

Is it my imagination, or has Mama Juju become even younger? When I first met her, she'd seemed to be in her sixties. Last evening she'd seemed younger, as though just having crossed the threshold of fifty. Today she seems barely a few years older than me. I blink and look at her carefully, but a sudden beam of bright sunlight falls upon her from the open door, obscuring her face from me. My eyes squint, trying to adjust to the difference. The shop seems cleaner, fresher almost, as though someone has applied a lick of paint to it. Still overcrowded, the bric-a-brac seems to have a semblance of order about it.

"Have you done something to the shop?"

She stares at me noncommittally. "Would you like another reading?"

Puzzled, I sit down. Something feels odd, as though I've stepped back in time.

"No, I don't want another reading. But do you have what I asked for?"

"Yes, they are here." She takes out a bulky package, wrapped in newspaper, tied with string and places it on the table. "Do you want to check?"

I nod, swallowing compulsively, my hands shaking as I gently unwrap the package.

The likeness is extraordinary! There they lie, my ex-boyfriend and my best friend, like two miniature versions of themselves condensed into these cloth dolls. The limbs are floppy, the smiles fixed upon their vacuous faces.

I breathe deeply then look up at her, my surprise and delight visible upon my face.

"This is amazing! It's wonderful. You are a genius."

Mama Juju nods and looks at me gravely. "Follow the instructions in the letter. You will get what you want."

"How much?"

I flinch at the figure she quotes, but quickly pull out the credit card I'd kept for this very purpose, one that I intend to shut down after this transaction is paid for. She flicks a crimson fingernail at it.

"Cash!"

"I'm not carrying that much on me ..."

She reaches out and pulls the package out of my hands.

"Then bring it!" Her eyes are mere slits, her mouth a straight line, and I can feel her anger reverberating around me. I jump up and hurry out, rushing to the bank, hoping I can withdraw the sum needed; hoping she doesn't change her mind in the interim.

. . .

Three hours later I return, carrying the cash in a bag that I grasp tightly under my arm. She looks up and smiles, her crooked teeth looking whiter than before.

I want to tell her how hard it was to withdraw the sum of money, how much explaining I had to do, the verification I had to provide, the accounts I had to empty, but something tells me she doesn't care.

Once again, she places the package before me. It is my turn to question her, my festering anger coming out in a single, cold question, reason having replaced rashness for now.

"How do I know this will work?"

She places her elbows upon the table, steepling her fingers together.

"You want to know if it will work?" Her voice is just above a whisper, but the menace is unmistakable.

"Yes," my voice quivers in response, "it is a lot of cash ..."

"Wait here!" She commands, standing up suddenly, towering over me. She gives me a scornful glance and walks away towards the back of the shop, her robes swishing noiselessly.

I wait quietly, all my old doubts resurfacing. What am I doing here? Is revenge really that important? Isn't it healthier to move on, to let destiny take me where it wills? Then I think of them: Will and Maddie, laughing together, their faces aglow in their engagement photograph and my anger returns unbidden. A searing headache declares my resolve. I clutch my head, moaning softly. Hate has hidden itself in every crevice of my body, resurfacing in the most unexpected ways. I scramble through my handbag, looking for my Tylenol, swallowing it down dry. And just as quickly, the headache disappears.

Mama Juju stands above me again, holding a glass of water.

"You have a strong constitution."

I look up, puzzled.

"Call her, your blonde friend. Call her now."

I pull out my cell phone and call Maddie, as instructed.

"Valentina!" She answers breathlessly, as though waiting for my call.

"Hi Maddie! Mama told me you'd called."

"Yes, I've been trying to get hold of you, but aaaahhhh ..." She screams suddenly.

"Are you okay?" I ask, concern lacing my words, concern that I cannot dispense with, no matter how much I hate her now. Then I look across and see Mama Juju twisting the doll's foot. The doll that looks like Maddie.

"My foot! I ... I don't know what I've done to it ... aaahhhhh ... Vallé, I ... I'll call you later ... aaahhhhh ..."

She hangs up.

Mama Juju keeps twisting the little foot, watching me intently. My forehead breaks out in beads of sweat.

"Stop," I whisper hoarsely. "Stop, please!"

She stops, placing the doll carefully upon the table.

"I do not promise that which I cannot deliver."

I nod slowly, realising that what I have started is well beyond my understanding. My apprehensions have solidified into fear. I pick up the package quietly and get up to leave.

"If I need to contact you again, how do I do it?"

Mama Juju sits back in the chair, her posture relaxed, looking younger than me now.

"Just think of me. I will come to you."

"Come to me? How?"

"Oh, do not worry about that Valentina. I will find a way."

I retrace my steps out, my mind unable to process what just happened. I walk back to the hotel, the package heavy in my hands. Can I really go through with this? It's one thing to want to inflict pain, quite another to actually do it. A thought nags at the edges of my mind, but I'm unable to articulate it, so I let it go.

It's 6:15 p.m. as I walk past the L bar. My eyes briefly glance at the lonely man nursing his drink and just for a moment I pause. Then I move on, unaffected.

Back in my room, I unwrap the dolls again and examine them thoroughly. To an outsider, they would look like little rag dolls, children's playthings. But I know the power that I wield over bodies and lives if I choose to use it. I turn them this way and that, trying to figure out how Mama Juju made them, that from hundreds of miles away she could elicit a reaction so powerful. Then I remember the instructions she has put down in the letter and look for it. It's a single page of lined paper with serrated edges, folded over into a tiny little chit. I lean back on the headstand of my bed, unfolding the chit slowly. Her writing is like a child's scrawl, almost illegible in parts, but the instructions are clear enough.

I want to do the first part straight away, but hesitate with the second. There is a tiny needle that was enclosed in the note. I take it out and prick my finger, as instructed. Then I hold it over the Will doll, letting the droplet of blood fall onto its chest, and watch it seep in, leaving no mark or stain behind. Every day, the instructions say, every day, till his heart is filled with you, only you.

The Maddie doll lies limp, her body half in and half out of the package that I'd placed on the bed. She watches me from a distance, as though assessing just how much damage I am going to inflict upon her little person. I close my eyes and breathe deeply. Can I do this? Can I really, really do this to the person I grew up with, shared music, clothes and confidences with? My mind recalls the instances of us sneaking into movie halls, one after the other, having paid to watch just one film but naughtily watching several. Our swearing each other to secrecy, smoking our first joint together, hiding behind the school library. Our double dates, our crushes, our shared excitement over our favourite sitcom 'Jane the Virgin'. Pizza, cold beer and magazines. Doing each other's nails and makeup. Snapchatting well into the night. They are all good memories. But one thing stands out distinctly to me now. Maddie has always taken from me. Whether it was money, time or my family's affection, she has always been a taker, never a giver. Yes, she comes from a fractured family, just marginally better-off than us, but it has never been in her heart or her nature to give. Her beauty and charm have eased the path for her in so many ways that she simply cannot see her own selfishness.

Taking the doll out I place her next to Will. With the same needle, I touch her chest lightly, just a tiny pinprick. It will do, for now.

I put them both back in the package and ready myself for bed. My flight is early tomorrow morning and it's straight to work from there. I change into my pyjamas, wash my face and brush my teeth, only momentarily allowing myself to notice the fine lines at the corners of my eyes. Crows feet, they call them. The stress of the last eighteen months have taken their toll on me.

As I climb beneath the covers, exhausted from the day's events, the elusive thought resurfaces. Mama Juju's face swims into view as she says, "Oh, do not worry about that Valentina. I will find a way."

How did she know my name?

The next morning, rushing through the airport, the answer comes to me. Of course! She must've spotted it on the credit card. I smile to myself, my paranoia is out of control.

As I settle into the window seat, watching dawn break in the horizon, I feel happier than I have ever felt. This is going to work, I feel it in my bones. My life is finally going to fall into place exactly how I envisaged it. The plane pushes back and I plug my earphones in. I am ready for a new beginning.

———

Mama Juju looks down at her hands, they are so much smoother now, the veins having flattened out beautifully, the crepiness having all but disappeared. It feels good to be young again, she thinks as she examines her face in the mirror, the skin supple, glowing with the remembered youth of her bygone days. Unwrapping the scarf from her head, she smiles to discover that the grey has gone completely. Her curls are as dark and springy as before.

She picks up the doll and flicks at her dark, chestnut hair, into which she has woven that single strand the owner had left behind on the chair she'd first sat on.

Oh yes, she was ripe for the plucking, her fire burning brightly even on that first night. Not like the other one, all limp and placid, with no strength, no charisma at all. For years she had looked for someone exactly like her; willing it, wishing it, wanting it with every bit of juju coursing through her veins. Then the girl had wandered in, giggling and drunk, paying to have her fortune read out to her while an invisible web wove itself tightly around her.

Mama Juju had waited patiently for the girl to return, knowing she would and knowing that each time she did, she would forfeit her youth, her glow, her very lifeblood to her, unknowingly.

Let her have what she wants. Let her be happy, because that happiness will come with a price attached. She will age and wither before her time, her victories will be hollow, her love bought and paid for. And she will live with the guilt of someone's blood on her hands; guilt that will eat at her daily until, looking for answers, for redemption, she will return again.

But Mama Juju will be long gone by then. Rejuvenated for another fifty years, her next victim only a pinprick of time away.

REARVIEW

She rummaged through the drawer, her panic increasing progressively.
It wasn't here either. She had looked everywhere she could possibly
have thought to put it inadvertently, unthinkingly. Now, she was
starting to look in the silly places - the refrigerator, shoe closet, paper-
work drawer, airing cupboard. She wasn't old enough to have lost her
marbles yet, but she certainly seemed to have lost her precious pearls.

Walter's pearls. The ones he'd bought her in Hong Kong when they
were posted there. In their early, heady days of marriage when gifts,
little and large, punctuated their idyllic existence. She had worn them
frequently at first, her natural elegance enhanced by the soft sheen of
the Akoya pearls that encased her lovely long neck. Then, as age began
its ravages on her face and body, she wore them less. Walter was home
less frequently too. It all seemed pointless after a while, after no children and far too many postings, and whispers of concubines.

Still, within those pearls lay wrapped her dreams and her memories,
which she couldn't bear to part with. Even when the medical costs
grew to the extent where most of her jewellery was swallowed up. Even
as they downsized and Walter's chairlift absorbed the last of their
savings, she'd held on to them. They were a surviving symbol of the

happy future she had envisaged as a giddy, young bride. And now, they were gone.

She looked at the mess strewn around her and sighed. It would take far too long to put right, and in her frame of mind, all she wanted was to retreat to her little garden and finish that bottle of Pinot Grigio she had chilling in the refrigerator. The setting sun was casting an orange glow into her room, and she looked down at her shaking hands, willing herself to be calm. She would return to her search tomorrow and the many endless tomorrows that would inevitably follow.

The first sip was a delicious invitation into oblivion. She knew she was in that twilight zone where just one more step would lead her into full-blown alcoholism. But after years of disciplined self-deprivation, she no longer cared. She looked around at her well-tended garden, with its neat hedgerows and potted plants that housed a profusion of colours, and smiled sadly. There was never anyone to share it with. After Walter, she had licked her wounds for far too long. Her self-inflicted hibernation had lost her the few friends she had. Now, except for the hawk-faced harridan that lived at number 10, she never came across anyone in her quiet cul-de-sac.

The wind had a slight chill to it and as it passed over her, she pulled her shawl closer. Smoke wafted over the fence, and she heard a wheezy cough. Cyril? Cecil? What was his name, she wondered. The reclusive widower that lived next door.

"Hello?" She called out, surprising herself.

There was a pause, and then a soft Scottish burr answered her equally hesitantly, "Hello?"

"I ... I was wondering if you'd like to join me for a glass of wine?" She said, once again surprised at her own temerity.

After two beats came the wonderment-tinged response, "Yes, I would very much like that."

She ran her fingers through her hair, and quickly tidied the cushions on the sofa, while mentally kicking herself for not applying any lipstick.

She yanked open the door on the first knock and he stood there with his hand still raised, the other hand leaning heavily on the cane. She quickly took in the patrician nose, the grey hair, the tweed jacket that had seen better days and smiled at him, slightly embarrassed by her open appraisal.

"Do come in." She turned to let him pass, at once noticing the limp.

In the garden, she learnt his name really was Stuart and that his wife had passed ten years ago. His sons and their families ignored him except for Christmas, when he was passed around like a well-used toy between them. He spoke without rancour, and she listened in sympathy.

"Martin lives fifteen minutes away. He is a GP. A very busy man. He drops in on me when he can. He doesn't tell Sue. Sometimes he stays for a wee dram."

His eyes lit up as he spoke of his younger son. Then he stopped and looked at her. Really looked at her. "And what about you, little lady? Why do you hide in here all day and all night? Why aren't you about, painting the town red?"

She laughed at him. "How old do you think I am Stuart? My days of painting anything red are long gone."

"Ach noh! To me, you are a spring chicken, too pretty to be gardening all day."

And drinking all night, she surmised from the way his eyes flicked to the nearly empty bottle and away.

"Would you like a refill?"

She returned with a bowl of peanuts, her rumbling stomach reminding her that dinner time had come and gone. Somehow, she didn't mind. This easy camaraderie was filling a different hunger.

He spoke of his youth in Inverness. She told him of her travels around the world. He talked of his hopes of Scotland finally gaining independence, the referendum he hoped would be passed against all odds. She described to him the hustle and bustle, the smell and the chaos of the Bombay fish markets. He talked of his beloved wife, Jane. She topped up their glasses, thought briefly of Walter, and spoke no more.

The crickets came out and the moths furiously circled the lamp in the garden. They sat together in silence until he reached across and put his hand over hers. The feel of his leathery palm dislodged something inside her. Her tears dampened the front of his jacket. Her gasping sobs interspersed with hiccupping sorries. Out came every worry, every silly and sad concern that had jostled for space inside her. The mislaid pearls, the mislaid self-esteem. His hand patted her back, smoothed her hair, muttered quiet soothing words she couldn't make out, till she felt herself melt into him, reaching out in the darkness, towards his lips. He pushed her back gently.

"I must leave now, m'dear. It is late."

She nodded; abashed, aroused, ashamed.

He let himself out. She staggered upstairs to bed, sleeping fitfully; her dreams a jagged landscape peopled with smoke and pearls and a wistful heaviness.

The next morning, she stumbled downstairs in search of water, the thudding behind her eyes threatening to reach epic proportions. A note was placed carefully on her sideboard. The handwriting on the note was unfamiliar, almost old fashioned.

Her befuddled mind could not understand how her pearls sat next to the note, so innocuously, giving nothing away.

Momentarily distracted by the loud noises next door, she thrust the note and her necklace into her dressing gown pocket and went out to investigate.

Paramedics, police, the ambulance, and a multitude of people were traipsing in and out of Stuart's house. Alarmed, she ran forward, to be briskly informed she couldn't enter. Only family was allowed.

A visibly shocked, pale-faced man walked out and spoke to the police officer. Martin, she guessed. She called out. "What's happened? Is Stuart all right?"

He looked at her and looked away, as though she didn't matter. She supposed she really didn't.

The hawk-faced woman from number 10 came over to her conspiratorially.

"He's dead. That's his son. Found him this morning. Heart attack, they are saying."

"Oh!" Her sharp intake of breath made the shrew pause briefly in her narrative.

With eager relish she continued. "Been dead a week at least, they say. Poor sod!"

The ground swam up to meet her.

Hours later, revived by the paramedics and treated for shock, she remembered the note. It lay crumpled in her pocket. She smoothened it, pulling her pearls out alongside. It said:

> *Thank you for last night. It was good to feel wanted again, to feel alive. I know you were looking for these and I found them for you. Wear them and live your life, little lady. It goes by far too quickly.*

The note fell from her shaking hands. Glancing up at the mirror above the mantelpiece, she saw that her face was ashen. Her mind felt numb, unable to comprehend how something that had felt so real, so true, might have only been a mirage.

Had she been teetering on the edge of insanity last night?

And yet ...

She looked down at the crumpled note, then at the pearls sitting in her hand like a coiled serpent. Slowly, and with an aching deliberateness, she let them drop to the floor.

THE END

Sign up today to hear of Poornima's new releases and promotions!

AFTERWORD

Word-of-mouth is crucial for any author to succeed and if you found this book interesting *please* do leave a review on your preferred retailer. Even if it's just a star rating or a sentence or two, it would make all the difference and would be very much appreciated!!

———

If you enjoyed this book, you can sign up to hear more about my new releases and any special offers!

Do visit www.poornimamanco.com to keep abreast of all my news.

ALSO BY POORNIMA MANCO

Parvathy's Well & other stories

Damage & other stories

Holi Moly! & other stories

The Intimacy of Loss

Parvathy's Well & Other Stories: The India Collection

A Quiet Dissonance

ACKNOWLEDGMENTS

Here I am again - at this juncture where I sit down and work out how many people it actually took to create this book. They say it takes a village to bring up a child. Pretty much the same way, a book is a team effort. Yes, the ideas may begin in my mind, but they find ultimate fruition through the input of several people.

Let me start with my Alpha team - my family. They are the first ones to be exposed to my nascent ideas. As they weigh in on what works or doesn't, I make changes accordingly. Then they know that I am lost to them for several weeks as I sit at my laptop day and night, tapping away, earphones plugged in, oblivious to the outside world. This is perhaps the perfect place to thank them for their love, their patience and understanding. You will have me back soon enough. That's a promise!

Once my initial draft is finalised, I send it across to my wonderful editor in Bengaluru. What a find she has been! For a long time, I struggled to find a professional editor who understood the many languages and dialects I like to incorporate in my stories. Charulatha doesn't just do that, she actually enhances all my little quirks by understanding exactly what I'm trying to convey. She and I are on such a perfectly aligned wavelength that sometimes we edit things on the fly, talking to each other on WhatsApp while making corrections to the draft along-side. She has my lifelong gratitude (and business!).

Then there is my fabulous ART (Advance Reader Team). They go through my penultimate draft with fresh eyes and find the errors and discrepancies that might have slipped through the initial edits. V, V, A, M, H - thank you for all that you do!

{If you'd like to be a part of my ART, drop me a line at poornima@poornimamanco.com.}

Team Miblart has once again brought a super cover to life. It's pretty tricky trying to create a cover for a book that has stories from all over the world. The only thing I could think of that represented this eclectic mix, this smorgasbord, was a box of chocolates, and look how well they designed that yummy box!

These stories are a bit like Forrest Gump's - "My mom always said life was like a box of chocolates. You never know what you're gonna get." Well, neither do you before you dip into a tale. I really hope you found each chocolate tasty.

Finally, this book is recognition of the wanderlust that resides within my soul. I love travelling. My job has been about travelling. In the course of my life and through all my travels, one indisputable fact has emerged - at the heart of it, we are all the same! Regardless of colour, provenance, language, region and education, we feel the exact same emotions. So, why the hate? Why the segregation? Why the divisiveness? But that is a debate for another day.

I really hope you enjoyed this book, and that you will consider joining me on my journey by picking up some of my other works too.

Many thanks and happy reading!

———

If you would like to contact Charulatha or Team Miblart, their details are as follows:

charu.dpp@gmail.com

team@miblart.com

ABOUT THE AUTHOR

Always a voracious reader, Poornima started writing at the age of eight and never really stopped, although there were many dry spells.

She found her writing voice in 2009 when a short story of hers placed in an online competition run by The Guardian newspaper. Having re-discovered her first love, she started an online blog where she continued to write articles and stories, many of which ignited thought-provoking debates and conversations.

In 2018, her stories appeared in two separate books as a part of the India trilogy. 'Holi Moly! & other stories', the third book in the trilogy was published early 2020.

Having lived half her life in India and half in the United Kingdom, besides having travelled the world extensively, she considers herself a global citizen. She is married and has two teenage daughters.

Made in the USA
Middletown, DE
23 September 2021